MONTANA MAVERICKS

Welcome to Big Sky Country, home of the Montana Mavericks! Where free-spirited men and women discover love on the range...

BROTHERS AND BRONCOS

Romance is in the air for the ranchers of Bronco, but someone is watching from the sidelines. A man from the town's past could be behind the mysterious messages, but does he pose a threat to Bronco's future? With their happily-ever-afters at stake, the bighearted cowboys will do what it takes to protect their beloved town— and the women they can't live without!

THE MAVERICK'S MARRIAGE PACT

Maddox John needs a honey in a hurry to gain control of the family ranch. Adeline Longsworth needs money in a hurry to start her dream business. The hardheaded groom and his convenient bride put on such a convincing act that even they start to believe it. But a deal is a deal, and there's no way either of them will admit what's really in their hearts...

Dear Reader,

Welcome to Bronco, Montana! Fall has cooled the mountain air, the leaves are red and gold, and fat orange pumpkins are dotting the fields. The holidays aren't far away, but before they arrive, the town is getting ready to celebrate the annual Bronco Harvest Festival. With plenty of food and games and hayrides offered for entertainment, the event always draws huge crowds eager to celebrate the fall season.

Maddox John doesn't normally partake in the town's festivities. Bobbing for apples or going for hayrides isn't his style. When he isn't working on his family ranch, the Double J, he prefers to be relaxing in some romantic spot with a drink in his hand and a woman in his arms. But Maddox's life has recently taken a sudden change. He's now engaged to beautiful Adeline Longsworth, and the Bronco Harvest Festival is the perfect outing to convince everyone his playboy days are over and that he's head over heels in love with his fiancée.

As a child, Adeline had always enjoyed playing pretend, but now that she's a grown woman and pretending to be in love with Maddox, the fun of playing make-believe is quickly losing its luster. Especially when she wants to believe the sexy cowboy's kisses are the real deal!

I hope you enjoy Maddox and Adeline's journey to finding real love and that this year and every year, your fall season is filled with warmth and happiness.

Best wishes,

Stella Bagwell

The Maverick's Marriage Pact

STELLA BAGWELL

HARLEQUIN

SPECIAL
EDITION

Special thanks and acknowledgment are given to Stella Bagwell for her contribution to the Montana Mavericks: Brothers & Broncos miniseries.

Recycling programs
for this product may
not exist in your area.

ISBN-13: 978-1-335-72419-9

The Maverick's Marriage Pact

Copyright © 2022 by Harlequin Enterprises ULC

For questions and comments about the quality of this book, please contact us at CustomerService@Harlequin.com.

Harlequin Enterprises ULC
22 Adelaide St. West, 41st Floor
Toronto, Ontario M5H 4E3, Canada
www.Harlequin.com

Printed in U.S.A.

After writing more than one hundred books for Harlequin, **Stella Bagwell** still finds it exciting to create new stories and bring her characters to life. She loves all things Western and has been married to her own real cowboy for forty-four years. Living on the south Texas coast, she also enjoys being outdoors and helping her husband care for the horses, cats and dog that call their small ranch home. The couple has one son, who teaches high school mathematics and is also an athletic director. Stella loves hearing from readers. They can contact her at stellabagwell@gmail.com.

Books by Stella Bagwell

Harlequin Special Edition

Men of the West

Her Kind of Doctor
The Arizona Lawman
Her Man on Three Rivers Ranch
A Ranger for Christmas
His Texas Runaway
Home to Blue Stallion Ranch

Montana Mavericks:
The Real Cowboys of Bronco Heights

For His Daughter's Sake

The Fortunes of Texas: The Lost Fortunes

Guarding His Fortune

Montana Mavericks: The Lonelyhearts Ranch

The Little Maverick Matchmaker

Visit the Author Profile page
at Harlequin.com for more titles.

To Susan Litman, our great Montana Maverick editor.

Thank you for making these stories extra special.

Chapter One

Maddox John needed to find himself a wife! And fast!

Although he didn't necessarily think he'd find the solution to his problem by staring at the squatty tumbler sitting on the bar in front of him, a few sips of the whiskey and soda might help him get more comfortable with the idea that was beginning to hatch in his brain.

Up until a few hours ago, the idea of him getting married for any reason was laughable. In fact, Maddox had laughed until his sides ached when his brother Jameson had told him about their father's edict: whichever one of his four children was the first to marry, in a style befitting the Johns' social standing, would inherit the greatest share of the Double J Ranch.

The whole notion was ludicrous, Maddox thought as a sip of the smooth whiskey slid down his throat. Having a lavish wedding to impress his friends and acquaintances around Bronco, Montana, was hardly a good reason for his father to change his will and decree that upon his death, the largest hunk of the family ranch would go to the first child to fulfill his wish. But Randall and Mimi John had always believed it was important to show everyone they were just as wealthy as any of the well-to-do families in and around Bronco. Particularly the Abernathys and the Taylors, two of the richest ranching families in the area.

Looking at the situation from a logical standpoint, most would say Randall could make the generous promise to his children simply to get what he wanted, then later renege on changing his will. But Maddox knew his father well. Randall never backed out of a deal. Once he made a promise, it was etched in stone.

Still, none of this would be happening if his brother Jameson and his fiancée would only agree to have the elaborate wedding ceremony his parents wanted. But they stubbornly refused, and the more Maddox thought about the whole issue, the more confident he felt about turning the regrettable situation into something profitable for himself.

Logically, though, Jameson had the best chance of fulfilling their parents' wishes. After all, he and Vanessa Cruise had been engaged for nearly ten months now. But Maddox couldn't completely rule out his other two siblings. Dawson, their younger brother at twenty-eight, was popular with the ladies, but he displayed no interest in settling down. Charity, the baby of the John family, was twenty and beautiful. She'd already drawn a long line of suitors and presently had a steady boyfriend rich enough to gain their parents' approval. But Maddox wasn't sure his sister or her boyfriend, Nick, were ready to tie the knot just to inherit a big hunk of the Double J.

So that left Maddox to give Jameson a run for his money—or, in this case, a run for the bulk of the ranch. But was he prepared to give up his freedom? And even if he was willing, where would he find a woman who'd agree to become Mrs. Maddox John?

At thirty, he'd already gone through a whole date-book of women. And though he'd enjoyed some sessions of red-hot passion with a few of those ladies, each relationship had quickly fizzled to nothing more than a pile of cool ashes. In fact, he couldn't begin to fathom falling wildly in love. No, Maddox was a rambling man, and knowing this about him, most of his old flames would never actually consider him husband material. But that hardly meant he couldn't find someone new in the Bronco social circle, he thought. A woman who'd be willing to marry him for all the wrong reasons.

Hell, she wouldn't have to be in love with him, he thought. She'd only have to pretend to be.

"Ready for another round? Looks like you could use it this evening."

Maddox looked up to see Rusty, the bartender at DJ's Deluxe. The middle-aged man with a shock of wavy red hair was usually a man of few words who kept his opinions safely to himself. Apparently, in Rusty's eyes, Maddox looked like a man with a troubled mind.

A wry twist on his lips, Maddox asked, "What makes you think I could use another drink?"

"The crease between your brows. I've never seen you with one of those, Mr. John."

Scowling, Maddox said, "Mr. John! Hell, Rusty, I'm Maddox to you. What's with the mister?"

The bartender grinned. "Nothing. It was just a test to see if you were actually listening. You are."

Maddox grunted. "You know, my parents would say that if a bartender knows you by your first name, you're drinking too much."

"Bah! I haven't seen you in this place for more than a week. So what brought you here tonight? Meeting a pretty lady?"

DJ's Deluxe was an upscale barbecue restaurant in Bronco Heights, the ritzy side of Bronco. It took a reservation to get a table for dinner, and Maddox had none. But he hadn't come in for barbecue—he'd come in for a drink and to contemplate his next step.

He'd never thought it fair that Jameson would eventually inherit the largest share of the ranch just because he was the eldest of the John siblings. Heck,

Maddox worked just as hard as his brother to make the Double J go. In his mind, he deserved equal rewards. But could he tolerate a wife to get his fair share? That was the most important question.

"No date for me tonight," Maddox answered Rusty's question. "I only drove into town for a drink and to get away from the ranch for a while."

Rusty nodded, then, spotting a customer taking a seat on a stool at the far end of the bar, he said, "Excuse me, Maddox. Duty calls."

The bartender moved away, and Maddox picked up his drink and thoughtfully rolled the cold glass between his palms.

Meeting a pretty lady. His wife wouldn't necessarily have to be a raving beauty, but Randall and Mimi would expect their daughter-in-law to be presentable and have a respectable reputation. And Maddox? Well, when it came to women, he wasn't fussy. To him, they were all pretty and presentable. As for their reputations, who was he to judge?

The cowboy sitting at the end of the bar was one hot dude. As soon as Adeline Longsworth sat down on the bar stool and ordered a martini, she'd noticed him.

How could a woman not notice a man like him? Even with his knees bent and the heels of his expensive cowboy boots hung over the foot rail of the bar stool, she could tell he was a tall, long-legged guy. A denim Western shirt stretched snugly across his broad chest and shoulders, while a black Stetson rested low on his forehead.

Beneath his hat, she could see his hair was a color caught somewhere between yellow corn silk and caramel brown. She could also see that his face boasted a strong, square jaw, a proud chin and a set of chiseled lips, while the hollows beneath his sharp cheekbones matched the lean lines of his body.

Occasionally she met her friend Trudy here at DJ's Deluxe for drinks and dinner. But she was certain she'd never seen this man during one of those visits. He was the sort a woman didn't forget.

The bartender served her drink, and as she took a tiny sip of the cold cocktail, she told herself it was a waste to take a second look at the man. For one thing, he probably had a wife and children at home. And secondly, even if he was single, her parents, Louis and Naomi, would never approve of her dating a cowboy. Which was the epitome of snobbery. The Lazy L, her parents' massive ranch, wouldn't be much without a crew of cowboys to handle the livestock and care for the land.

But Adeline didn't want to think about her parents tonight. Especially the hand they'd had in pushing Spence out of her life. She didn't have concrete evidence to prove it, but she'd be willing to throw down a huge bet that Louis had put some sort of pressure on her boyfriend to make sure he disappeared from his daughter's life.

"Mind if I join you?"

The deep male voice jerked Adeline out of her miserable thoughts, and she turned her head to see the sexy cowboy throwing a leg over the stool next to hers.

Surprised but doing her best to hide it, she gave him a cool little smile. "Not at all. I thought you looked a little lonely down there."

One corner of his hard lips curved upward. "You noticed?"

Darn it, now why had she let that slip out? No doubt he was thinking she'd been sitting here eyeing him.

"Well, it was obvious that no one else was sitting near you," she answered.

A full-blown smile spread across his face, and her gaze was drawn to the faint dimples creasing his cheeks and the laugh lines fanning out from the corners of his eyes.

"I couldn't help but notice that no one else was sitting next to you, either," he said.

Oh my. From a distance she'd thought he looked sexy, but now that the space between them had been narrowed down to a few inches, she was finding it hard to breathe, much less stop herself from staring.

His eyes were blue. Not the icy color, but like a blue flame burning everything within its reach. And at this very moment, Adeline was definitely feeling the heat.

Her fingers unconsciously tightened around the

stem of her glass. "I'm—uh—waiting for a friend. We have dinner reservations."

"I see. So you're relaxing with a drink before he arrives."

"*She*. My friend is an old schoolmate."

Was that a glint she saw in his eyes? Or was she seeing a reflection of the candle flickering on a shelf behind the bar? Either way, the warm light was totally disarming.

"That's nice," he said.

Ice cubes clinked as he gently swished the amber-colored liquid in his glass. At the same time, his gaze was making a lazy survey of her face, and Adeline was suddenly imagining the feel of his fingertips following the same track his eyes had taken over her cheeks and lips.

The illicit thoughts prompted her to take a long swig of her drink and hope the mixture of gin and vermouth would dull her out-of-control senses.

"By the way, I'm Maddox John," he introduced himself. "My family owns the Double J north of town."

John! She turned wide eyes on him. "Oh. I recognize the name."

A frown tugged his brows together. "We've met before?"

"I don't believe so. But I recall my father having a feud with the John patriarch over a government contract. It happened a few years ago."

He hardly appeared put off by the fact that their

fathers had once been on the outs with each other. He actually looked more amused than anything.

"And who is your father?" he asked.

"Louis Longsworth. He owns the Lazy L Ranch. I'm Adeline, his eldest daughter."

He extended his hand to her. "Nice to meet you, Adeline."

"My pleasure, Maddox." She placed her hand in his and was instantly rattled by the warmth of his strong fingers.

"To tell you the truth," he said, "my father has been in more feuds than I'd like to admit or can possibly remember. Whatever the fuss between our parents, I'm glad you're not holding it against me."

His fingers tightened slightly around hers as he spoke the last few words, and Adeline wondered if he was flirting with her or if the subtle response had merely been a reflex.

She said, "I think it involved government grazing land and actually, my father won the grant, so I'm pleased that you're not harboring ill feelings toward us Longsworths."

"Not at all," he said. "Besides, I have the feeling that you're in the same boat as me and my siblings. We can't control or even condone some of the things our fathers do."

She gently extricated her hand from his and purposely picked up her drink. Maybe the coolness of the glass would erase the warmth lingering in her fingers.

"Unfortunately, you are so right," she said tightly.

He looked at her. "You sound angry."

"That's because I am. For the past couple of weeks, I've been very upset with my parents for—" She broke off suddenly as it dawned on her that she was about to spill a private part of her life to this man. But what the heck if she did tell him about Spence? She doubted she'd ever see Maddox John again. "I'm twenty-five years old, but they still want to control me and butt into my personal life."

His lips took on a wry slant. "Causing trouble, huh? Parents have a way of doing that."

She lifted the green olive from her drink and popped it into her mouth. "Spence and I were getting on great. We liked a lot of the same things and never ran out of things to talk about. We enjoyed each other's company and were very compatible. But he just wasn't good enough for the daughter of a Longsworth. I don't know exactly what my parents did or said to chase him away, but I'm positive they're the reason he suddenly called it quits with me."

"That's not good."

"You darn well know it's not good!" she muttered.

For a moment she thought he was going to smile, but he must have decided she might be offended, because the tiny tug at the corners of his mouth quickly disappeared.

"Have you tried talking with your boyfriend about the problem?"

Shaking her head, she finished the last of her

drink and placed the glass on the bar. "When I said my parents must have chased him away, I meant it literally. Spence didn't just end our relationship, he moved to California."

"Oh. Sounds like it's really over."

Adeline's gaze dropped to her lap. She hoped Maddox John couldn't see the humiliation and pain she'd been dealing with these past couple of weeks. Throughout the whole experience, she'd been telling herself it was probably for the best that Spence was out of her life. A man who couldn't stand up to her father would hardly make a strong, dependable husband. Not that she'd been that serious about the guy. But she had enjoyed dating him. Now she felt awful because her parents had bullied him completely out of the state.

"Yes," she grimly replied. "It's over. Kaput."

The bartender appeared from nowhere to collect her empty glass.

"Would you like another, miss?" he asked.

"Bring her another of the same," Maddox told him. "My treat."

Adeline started to protest. "Thanks, but I'd better not. I—"

"Nonsense," he interrupted. "Your friend hasn't arrived yet. You need something to do while you wait."

There was something she needed to do, all right, Adeline told herself. She needed to get up and walk away from this cowboy who reminded her of a cool alley cat. Rough, tough and full of cocky confidence, he was definitely dangerous. But really, how much trouble could she get into by merely sitting on the bar stool next to him?

"Okay," she said with a nod to the bartender. "You talked me into it."

Maddox smiled, and as he twisted his stool slightly toward hers, Adeline caught the faint scent of prairie grass and something else that was utterly male. Just like the rest of him.

"So do you come here to DJ's Deluxe often?" he asked.

She crossed her legs and adjusted the cuff of her white blouse and wondered why he was putting her nerves on edge. She wasn't a schoolgirl. She'd dated a number of men. Some of whom had been very attractive. So why was this one playing havoc with her senses?

"Not often. And especially not on a weeknight. I have to be at work by nine, and my commute takes at least twenty minutes. More in the winter when the roads are snowy."

"What do you do?"

She took plenty of unwarranted criticism and daydreamed about having a business of her own, she wanted to say. Instead, she said, "I work as a travel agent for a sporting goods company—Peak Experience Sports, to be exact. I book all the travel for the executives and higher-ups."

He looked at her with interest. "Peak Experience

Sports is a huge company. Obviously the execs travel enough to keep you busy."

"I rarely have a spare moment," she confessed. "There's always some sort of convention or trade show or out-of-state business meeting going on. And, of course, all that work deserves plenty of vacations. I book hotel stays on tropical beaches or snowy ski resorts and wonder if I'll ever get a chance to have my own relaxation."

The bartender arrived with the fresh martini, and she promised herself she wouldn't drink more than half of it. Otherwise, she'd be saying anything and everything to this man.

"I can't remember the last time I've really gotten away from the ranch," he said. "There's always so much to do. And Dad—well, let's just say I know how you feel about your parents interfering in your private life."

Surprised, she looked at him. "Don't tell me you have the same problem. My father only has daughters, so it's second nature for him to try to boss us around. But it's hard for me to imagine your father trying to control his grown sons."

"Yeah, thirty is definitely grown-up. But Dad wouldn't let a little thing like age stop him from handing out rules and orders. In fact, he came up with a humdinger today."

More interested than she had a right to be, Adeline reached for her drink. "Surely he didn't order you to stop seeing a woman or chase her away with a threat," she said, her voice loaded with sarcasm.

"No. If you ask me, it's something worse. He's using his children as pawns to get what he and Mom want."

She grimaced. "Sounds like our fathers drank from the same watering hole."

He chuckled, and she smiled.

"You might be right," he joked. "Or could be when they had the feud over the land grant, their domineering ways rubbed off on each other."

She sipped the cocktail and wondered if it was him or the alcohol causing the strange vibration somewhere in her head.

"You mentioned that your father is using his children," she said. "Exactly what is he trying to do?"

He snorted. "Impress all his friends and acquaintances. Prove to them and the whole Bronco community that he has as much money and high social standing as anyone in the area."

"And how does he plan to accomplish this through his kids?"

He rolled his eyes. "Give one of them the most dazzling wedding that money can buy."

She laughed. "And that's a problem? Sounds wonderfully generous to me."

"Well, yes, to some couples it would be. But my brother Jameson and his fiancée, Vanessa, want a small, intimate ceremony. Lavish is not my brother's style, and Vanessa is far from the showy sort. They refuse to go along with Mom and Dad's wishes for an over-the-top wedding."

"Well, if small and intimate is what your brother and his fiancée want, then that's what they should have. After all, it's their wedding. But as for me, I'm just the opposite. When I get married, I want the most ostentatious wedding I can possibly have. You know, a fabulous bridal gown, huge wedding party, top-shelf liquor, ice sculptures, a sea of flowers and a live band to play at the reception—where the dancing would go on for hours. A woman gets married only once in her life—hopefully. She deserves to feel like a princess on that day."

A sinful little grin suddenly twisted his lips. "I don't know if I could manage to make you feel like a princess for a day, but I could treat you like royalty for one night," he said in a lowered voice.

Before Adeline could stop herself, she was laughing in his face. "Sorry if I choke on the cheese. Does that line usually work for you?"

He chuckled, and she had to smile. It was nice to run into a man with a sense of humor, she thought. One who didn't take himself so seriously.

"I don't know," he confessed. "I've never used it before."

"Good thing. Just between the two of us, you need to come up with something else."

She turned her attention back to her drink, and as she took a tiny sip, she could feel him studying her face.

Now what could he possibly be thinking—and what in the world was keeping Trudy? She desperately needed her friend to show up and give Adeline the excuse to leave the bar. She was getting too friendly with Maddox John. Especially when she could tell just by looking at the guy that he was the love 'em and leave 'em sort.

"Adeline, what would you say if I told you I could get you the wedding of your dreams?"

The question was so far-fetched she started laughing again. But as she noticed the look on his face was serious, her laughter faded to a smile.

"Okay," she had to ask. "What's the catch?"

"Well, the first stipulation is that you'd have to get married soon. Very soon. And the second—you'd have to marry me."

This time her laughter was practically hysterical, and as she tried to smother it behind her hand, she glanced around to see if anyone was noticing the exchange between her and Maddox. Currently, there was only one other person sitting at the bar, an older gentleman who was absorbed in the basketball game playing on the flat-screen TV on the wall behind the bar. Several diners were enjoying their meals, but they were too far away to pick up on their conversation. And though the bartender could probably hear them, he appeared to be ignoring them.

Lowering her voice, she said, "I've never heard of anything so crazy! Why would I agree to something as fantastic as marrying you? We only met a few minutes ago."

"I noticed." He shrugged, then lifted his hat from his head and ran a hand through thick waves of dark blond hair. "And now that we've talked a bit, I have a feeling you'd be the perfect wife for me."

This was turning out to be the strangest encounter she'd ever had with a man, Adeline thought, and it was getting weirder by the moment. "I suppose I should be flattered," she told him. "But honestly, I'm thinking I should have the bartender call for medical help. You're clearly in need of it."

This woman was hardly a pushover, Maddox thought as he levered his hat back onto his head. And to make her even more perfect, she was incredibly beautiful.

Slender to the point of appearing fragile, she made the crisp white blouse and black pinstriped slacks she was wearing look as though she'd just stepped off a Paris runway. Her dark brown hair was long and hung straight against her back, while her eyes were a warm brown that glowed against her pale complexion. He wanted to say her eyes were the most dazzling feature of her face, but he had to admit her full, bow-shaped lips were close to tying for that honor.

"Don't worry," he joked. "I get over these spells."

"You mean you don't normally go around proposing marriage to women you hardly know?"

He chuckled. "You happen to be the first. And if

you'll listen to my cause, I think you might be interested in tying the knot with me."

"Oh, sure. I've always had the wish to marry a man on a whim. The traditional way of acquiring a husband is far too boring for me," she said with a heavy dose of sarcasm. "You know, things like dating, getting to know your future spouse, falling in love. Totally unnecessary in my book."

There wasn't a single one of his old girlfriends who would've given him such a flippant reply, Maddox thought. And if she had, it would have rubbed him the wrong way. But with Adeline, he found the sassy attitude refreshing.

"Look, I understand this sounds outrageous. But when you hear the details, you might decide it's a profitable opportunity."

"You're right about one thing—your proposition does sound crazy. This might sound corny to you, but my plan is to marry for love, not profit."

He shook his head. "Love is fickle. In my opinion, you ought to be marrying for fun. Or to spite your father. Or to make a pile of money. You mentioned exotic vacations. Well, marrying me would enable you to enjoy plenty of those. Or set up your own financial security—away from your parents."

"And what would I have to do to earn this money? Jump through burning hoops? Or stick my head in a lion's mouth?"

"Nothing nearly so dangerous. In fact, you wouldn't have to do anything that you felt was wrong or made you uncomfortable. Ours would be a marriage of convenience. Nothing more."

Something indefinable flickered in her brown eyes before her long black lashes lowered and momentarily hid whatever she was thinking.

"Sorry. No way. Not interested."

Her response disappointed him, but only for a moment. When Maddox decided he wanted something, he didn't give up until he had it. And he wasn't about to give up on Adeline Longsworth becoming the wife he desperately needed.

He jotted his cell number on the corner of a napkin, and after tearing it off, he handed her the piece of vital information.

"Well, keep this, will you? Just in case you change your mind," he added with a provocative grin.

Just as she dropped it into her handbag and closed the latch, a woman's voice said, "Adeline, are you— Oh, you didn't tell me you were bringing a date tonight."

Maddox looked beyond Adeline's shoulder to see a petite young woman with wavy red hair standing a few steps away. From the look of surprise on her face, she must have already jumped to the conclusion that he was Adeline's date.

"Hello, Trudy," Adeline greeted, then darted a glance at him. "This is Maddox John. And we're— Uh, it's a bit complicated. Right?"

He flashed her a wide smile. "Yes, but not too complicated," he answered.

She cast him an enigmatic smile, then slid off the bar stool and quickly grabbed hold of the red-head's arm. "Come on, Trudy. Let's see if our table is ready."

Maddox watched Adeline walk away before he twisted the stool back to the bar and motioned for Rusty to refill his glass.

"Don't tell me you struck out with Ms. Longs-worth," Rusty said with wry humor.

Surprised that the bartender knew Adeline's name, Maddox looked at him. "You know her?"

Rusty splashed whiskey and soda into Maddox's glass. "The only thing I know is that she's from the ultrawealthy Longsworth family. She and a good-looking young guy used to come in here together. But I haven't seen him around for a while."

"No. And you won't, either," Maddox said matter-of-factly. "From now on, I'm the guy you're going to see with Ms. Longsworth."

The bartender arched an inquisitive brow at him. "Really? How are you going to manage that?"

Maddox grinned. "Simple. I'm going to marry her."

Chapter Two

"Do you have a doctor's appointment, Maddox?"

Maddox glanced over at his younger brother, Dawson, as the two men stood at the hitching rail unsaddling the horses they'd been riding for the bigger part of morning.

"Where is that question coming from?" Maddox asked. "Do I look sick?"

"No. But you keep checking your watch like you have an important meeting on your agenda."

Damn. He didn't realize he'd been watching the time that closely or that he'd been so obvious about it.

"Checking on the cows and calves on the back range was the important thing on my to-do list today," Maddox said. "And we just finished that job."

Dawson grimaced. "I'm surprised Dad didn't order us to go to the west pasture with some of the hands and start tearing out the cross fence he wants rebuilt."

"Don't worry, we'll get that order tomorrow," Maddox replied. "While Jameson gets the honor of going with Dad to pick out a new bull to purchase."

Dawson grunted. "No surprise there. He values Jameson's opinion on cattle much more than he does ours. Heck, he lets Jameson have a say in most all the important decisions made around here. I don't ever remember him asking you or me what cows we should cull or the kind of hay we should feed."

Maddox didn't miss the resentment in Dawson's voice and he had to admit there were times he begrudged their father always setting Jameson on a lofty perch. But Maddox loved the ranch and, as far as he was concerned, he was working for its welfare, not Randall's.

"Well, it's not Jameson's fault that Dad views him in a special light," Maddox said. "Our brother doesn't ask for the royal treatment, so we can hardly blame him."

"I guess not," Dawson replied. "I only wish— well, that things around here could be a little fairer. You know what I mean?"

"Sure. But whining isn't going to change anything. Besides, today is a beautiful day. We need to enjoy what's left of it," Maddox told him. "And I've been tossing around the idea of driving into town to pick up something at the feed store."

Dawson shot him a sardonic smirk. "Like what? The pretty blonde that works in the office?"

Maddox lifted the left fender of the saddle and placed it on the seat before he began to loosen the front girth. "Pretty blonde? As in young and pretty? I wasn't aware that Brady Sellars had gotten rid of Gertie. She's done his books at Bronco Feed and Ranch Supply ever since Jameson and I were little boys."

"Gertie is still there. She needed help, so Brady hired another woman. I'm surprised you haven't noticed. Kathy is quite a looker."

Maddox grunted with amusement. "Sure sounds like you've noticed."

"I'd have to be wearing a blindfold not to notice. Even though she won't even look in my direction. But that's okay. One of these days she will. I'm going to make darn sure she does."

Dawson's vow wasn't far off from the one Maddox had made to himself last night as he'd driven home from DJ's Deluxe. He'd promised himself that one way or the other, he was going to persuade Adeline Longsworth to marry him. In fact, he'd been fairly certain he'd done a good job of pitching his idea to her.

When she'd walked away from him last night, there had been something on her face that said the two of them weren't finished; they were only getting started. But now that it was past noon and he hadn't heard one word from her, his confidence was clinging to a slippery slope. He was beginning to wonder if the subtle glint he'd spotted in her brown eyes and the provocative curve to her lips had only been a figment of his imagination.

Damn it, he'd spent most of last night and all this morning thinking about the dark-haired beauty with the saucy smile and tinkling laugh. Everything about her would make him a perfect wife. He had to make her see that the two of them would be a power couple.

Maybe you ought to think about making her see that you'd be a perfect husband, Maddox. What good is money if she has to put up with a jerk to get it?

Doing his best to ignore the taunting voice in his head, Maddox looked over at his brother. "Tell you what, Dawson, now that I've heard about this pretty blonde, I think you should make the trip to the feed store."

Dawson turned away from his horse to stare at Maddox in disbelief. "You're joking, right?"

He grinned. "No, I'm serious. You can pick up a tub of calf supplement as well as I can. And who knows, with a little luck you might talk Kathy into going on a date with you."

Maddox lifted the saddle from the horse and carried it into the tack room. Dawson slung his own saddle onto his shoulder and followed closely behind him.

"Okay, Maddox, what's the deal? I've never known you to miss a trip into town."

"There's no deal. I have a few other things to do anyway." He placed the saddle on a wooden stand, then walked over to his brother. "I imagine by now you've heard about Dad's wedding plan?"

Dawson's snort was a mixture of amusement and sarcasm. "You mean his wedding bribe, don't you?"

"Hmm. Wedding bribe. That might be a more accurate description," Maddox replied, then cautiously waited for Dawson to say more. He already knew Jameson's feelings about their father's plan to alter the inheritance of the ranch, but Maddox didn't have a clue as to how his two younger siblings felt about the idea.

"If you want to know what I think—the whole thing stinks," Dawson stated flatly. "It's just one more way Dad is trying to control us kids. But frankly, I don't care what he does about his will. I'm third in line to you and Jameson. My slice won't amount to much, anyway. Besides, I wouldn't get married for all the money in Bronco Bank and Trust. I have too much living to do to tie myself down with a wife."

Normally, Maddox would be thinking the same thing. He didn't want to be tied down, either. But he did want the major portion of the Double J. It was a prime piece of property. A true cattle empire. It was also the single most important thing in Maddox's life.

He doubted anyone in his family had ever recognized Maddox's deep love for the ranch. His parents and siblings all saw him as a guy whose main objective in life was having fun and dating a new woman every week. And Maddox supposed he'd given them good reason to view him in that manner. He'd never felt comfortable with letting anyone see the serious side of him, so he'd always hidden it behind a good-time image.

"I imagine Charity feels as you do," Maddox said in the most casual voice he could summon. "She's so young. And I honestly can't see her staying here on the ranch for the rest of her life."

Dawson shrugged. "She's too infatuated with Nick right now to care much about anything else."

"Infatuated enough to marry him, you think?" Maddox asked.

"Charity is fickle. It's hard to predict what she'll do about anything. Why do you ask? Worried about her making a mistake?"

For one split second, Maddox felt a bit ashamed of himself. If he truly was a thoughtful and loving brother, he'd be considering his siblings' prosperity rather than his own. But didn't a guy have to look out for his own interest once in a while? Otherwise, he'd never get ahead in life. He'd always be giving instead of taking, he mentally argued.

"When it comes to Dad, I worry about all of us making a mistake," he said and hoped his evasive answer would be enough to satisfy Dawson.

"You need to forget the whole thing, Maddox.

One way or the other, Jameson has this all locked up. Even if he refuses to have a big wedding, he's still the eldest son."

"So what? Dad doesn't like his wishes to be denied. If he gets disgusted enough, he'll slice up shares of the ranch any way he wants," Maddox retorted.

"Yeah, he could. That's why I don't intend to let him dangle any kind of bait over me." He leveled an amused look at Maddox, then burst out laughing. "Hey, I just got a great idea, brother. You could get married. The reign of Bronco's number one playboy would end, but you'd have your hands on the majority of the Double J."

Dawson had no clue just how close he was to the plan Maddox had already devised in his mind. And he wasn't about to reveal it to him or anyone in his family. To make his strategy work, everything would have to look genuine, not contrived for financial reasons.

"Yeah, maybe I could." Forcing himself to chuckle, Maddox jerked his thumb toward the open doorway. "Come on. Let's go to the house and get some lunch."

More than an hour later, after they'd consumed a plate of sandwiches, Dawson left for town and Maddox headed back to the barn with intentions of saddling a fresh mount. However, the closer Maddox got to the big barn, the more he decided he needed to talk with the one person who understood him better than anyone, his longtime friend Weston Abernathy.

Pulling a cell phone from his shirt pocket, Maddox redirected his route and walked over to where an octagon-shaped bench was built around a huge shade tree. After taking a seat on the worn wood, he scrolled through the contact list until he reached his friend's number, then punched it and hoped he hadn't caught the man at a busy time.

Weston was one of five Abernathy brothers, all of whom helped their father run the Flying A Ranch, a large cattle spread located some twenty minutes away from the Double J. Last year, Wes's brother Tyler had become engaged to Callie Sheldrick, while another brother, Dean, had also become engaged to Susanna Henry. Now, much to Maddox's dismay, Wes had fallen prey to the love bug and had slipped a sparkling engagement ring on Everlee Roberts's finger. The Abernathy bachelors were quickly falling to the wayside.

"Hey, Maddox, good to hear from you," Wes greeted. "What's up?"

"Do you have a minute to talk?"

"Sure, I have a few minutes. I'm waiting on Tyler and Dean to get back from working on a windmill."

"Great. We haven't talked in a few days. Now that you're engaged to Evy and soon to be daddy to little Lola, you don't have time for your old buddy," Maddox teased. "But that's okay. As long as you're happy."

Wes's chuckle was smug. "I never thought I could be this happy, Maddox. Crazy, isn't it? No one knows more than you how I used to be—footloose and fancy-free, with plenty of lovely women on my contact list. Now I can't imagine myself with any woman except Evy."

"If you ask me, it's darn scary." Maddox rested his back against the tree trunk. "I mean, I can sort of picture Tyler and Dean settling down with one woman. But not you."

Wes chuckled. "One of these days you'll get what it's all about, Maddox. You'll find *the* one, and then your rambling ways will truly end."

Maddox thoughtfully stroked a finger down the side of his face. "Actually, Wes, I'm thinking of ending the rambling for a while. In fact, that's partly the reason I called you. To see what you thought about the idea."

His friend let out another short laugh. "What does *for a while* mean? You plan to be serious only for a certain amount of time? What woman would put up with that? Unless— Well, I suppose you know a few women who'd be happy to have a short affair and then say goodbye."

Maddox grimaced. "That's not exactly what I'm thinking."

"Oh, you must be planning to swear off dating for a few months. Well, I think you might have a good idea. Abstinence will help clear your head and let you see the error of your ways."

Rolling his eyes at Wes's old-fashioned reaction, Maddox said, "I'm not thinking in those terms, either. I'm thinking I'm going to get married—as fast as I can."

"What?" Wes practically yelled the word. "Did you say *married*?"

"I did." He quickly explained the statute his father had come up with to force one of his children into having an elaborate wedding. "Dawson has called the whole thing a wedding bribe, and he's right. What Dawson—and the rest of my family—doesn't know is that I intend to make the most of Dad's offer. I've already presented the idea to a certain lady, and unless I'm reading her wrong, I believe she's seriously considering my offer. At least, I'm hoping she's going to go along with my plan."

Wes's loud groan reverberated through Maddox's ear.

"Have you lost your mind, Maddox? That's the most horrible idea I've ever heard of! Marriage isn't a game. And it sure shouldn't be entered into for financial gain!"

Maddox grimaced. On the surface, Wes's philosophy was probably right. But Maddox had never been a conventional man. He went at life differently, and he felt damn good doing it his own way. "Maybe not for you, Wes. But for me, this is a perfect setup."

"Perfect? Think about it, Maddox! What if you get hitched with this woman and then find someone you really love? Or what if she falls in love with some other guy and wants her freedom? If anything like that happened, you'd both be miserable."

Maddox smiled. "You're worrying for nothing, Wes. This isn't going to be a real marriage with feelings or fidelity factoring into things. It'll be a business arrangement in the guise of a marriage. We'll put on an outward show of love for our family and friends, but in reality we'll be faking it."

Wes's response was a muttered curse word. "How long do you think you can keep up that act?"

"I figure a year will be enough time to get the ranch signed over to me. After that, we'll get a quiet divorce. I'll pay my ex a nice sum of money for playing her part, and I'll own the major share of the Double J. It's a win-win situation all around."

"And your parents? What are they going to think when you and Mrs. John divorce so soon?"

Maddox let out a mocking snort. "They won't think anything—except that my wife and I couldn't get along. We tried, but our differences were too great." He chuckled slyly. "Besides, all they want is a big, showy wedding to impress their friends and fellow ranchers. They won't care if they lose a daughter-in-law. Anyway, who expects a marriage to last nowadays?"

"I darned well do!" Wes exclaimed. "When Evy and I say our vows, we mean for them to last forever. And I think this plan of yours is downright awful. It's hard to imagine any well-meaning woman going along with a sham marriage. You must have scraped the bottom of the barrel to find this one."

For some ridiculous reason, Maddox bristled at Wes's insinuation. Adeline Longsworth was a class act. She was hardly a scheming gold-digger! At least, she didn't come across to Maddox that way. "Far from it. She's a lovely woman."

"Then why do you want to corrupt her?" Wes shot the question back at him.

Maddox let out a rough sigh. "Look, ole buddy of mine, maybe you consider what I'm doing deceitful, but in truth, I'm only trying to get my rightful share of the ranch. Don't you agree that I've always worked as hard or harder than anyone else on the Double J?"

After a pause of silence, Wes said, "Okay, I have to agree with that. You've worked your rear off above and beyond what should be expected of any man. And I'm not trying to judge you, Maddox. I'm just afraid you're going to get hurt. I wouldn't want that to happen."

Maddox swiped a hand over his face while thinking this whole conversation could be for naught, anyway. If Adeline didn't come through for him, he'd be sunk. Because sometime between last night and this morning, he'd come to the decision that if he couldn't have her for a pretend wife, he was going to forget the whole idea.

"I don't want that to happen, either," he told Wes. "That's why I plan to be very careful."

* * *

"Adeline, I need you to change the dates on my trip to LA from the third week of November to the second week. I forgot about Thanksgiving. Company headquarters will be closed a few days for the holiday, and most of the executives will be leaving town."

Adeline tried not to grit her teeth as the VP of marketing barked instructions at her over the phone jammed to her ear. Only yesterday she'd tried to remind Mr. Gentry that Thanksgiving might interfere with his plans, but he'd refused to let her get a word in edgewise. Now she had dozens of cancellations to make, along with booking new reservations.

Her job managing travel for Peak Experience Sports was something her parents had practically pushed her into three years ago, not long after she'd graduated college. At that time, working for the sports company hadn't exactly been what she was looking for, but she'd been fortunate to find a job close to home. And anyway, she'd been thinking she'd be married and raising children sooner rather than later.

Unfortunately, that plan hadn't worked out. Not for lack of trying, she thought dully. She'd had plenty of boyfriends who ultimately would've proposed marriage—if her parents hadn't gotten in the way. As for her job here at Peak Experience Sports, it was becoming harder and harder not to quit. Especially when she knew that half the office staff resented

Adeline being on the payroll. In their opinion, she was rich and there were other women out there who needed the job more than her.

"I understand, Mr. Gentry. I'll have the new reservations ready shortly," she promised.

"Good. And once you're finished, Adeline, I'd like the itinerary sent to my desk."

"Of course. Would you prefer that in paper form or email? Or both?" Adeline asked, careful to keep her voice crisp and professional.

"Both. And, Adeline, be sure that the flight times aren't inconvenient. I don't want to have to get up at five in the morning in order to catch a plane."

Getting up at five would take major effort from a man who often showed up late for work, even though he didn't have to be there until nine thirty in the morning, Adeline thought with disgust.

"Certainly, Mr. Gentry," she told him. "I'll make sure you have plenty of time for breakfast and lounging."

"Perfect."

The phone clicked dead in her ear, and Adeline refrained from slamming the receiver on its hook. Not with Brenda, a thirty-year-old divorcée, sitting at a nearby desk watching her every move. Brenda, along with several other female employees, enjoyed gossiping about Adeline. Being young and rich and somewhat attractive made her a target for undeserved comments.

Doing her best not to dwell on the negative working conditions, Adeline got busy dealing with the reservations for the Los Angeles trip.

By the time she finished the task and delivered the itinerary to Mr. Gentry's desk, she was grateful to see it was time for her break.

Leaving the block of marketing offices, she made her way to the restroom, which was located down the corridor from the break room, her next stop for a quick cup of coffee.

She definitely needed something to perk her up, she thought. After the odd encounter she'd had with Maddox John last night at the bar in DJ's Deluxe, she'd been so consumed with thoughts of the man and his proposal, she'd barely managed to sleep a total of two hours. To make matters worse, when the alarm had jarred her awake this morning, he'd been the first thing to pop into her mind. And so far today, he was still stubbornly stuck front and center in her mind. Daydreaming about his rugged appearance, the sound of his voice, the lithesome way he'd moved and the erotic scent that had wrapped around him was making it nearly impossible to focus on her work.

She might as well admit it—the man had caused her senses to go a bit haywire. And the last thing she needed was to fall into the arms of a local lothario. Not that she knew for certain that Maddox John was a playboy, but with those eyes and that grin, she'd be willing to bet he'd bedded half the young women in Bronco. Still, just thinking of letting him slip a wedding ring on her finger was enough to send a shiver down her spine.

Trying to push the jumbled thoughts from her mind, Adeline stepped into the large restroom and quickly locked herself into the first empty stall she could find.

Moments later, she heard footsteps and voices entering the restroom.

"Did you see the dress she's wearing today? I wouldn't attempt to pull off anything so revealing. Especially here at work," one of the women said in a snarky tone.

Adeline cringed as she recognized the voice of Luella, a young woman who worked in customer service. Anytime Adeline crossed her path, Luella gave her a catty look. But so did most of the other women who worked in the office.

Stock-still, Adeline considered her choices. She could walk out of the stall and confront them face-to-face, or she could stay put and suffer silently through the rest of their trashy gossip.

Deciding to take the coward's way out, she remained behind the stall door.

"Okay, Princess Longsworth has the right body to wear that kind of clingy garment," another woman replied in a sarcastic voice. "But that slit up the side of the skirt belongs in a nightclub, not at work."

Luella laughed slyly. "Uh, that depends on the type of work."

Adeline looked down at the printed black-and-beige dress she was wearing. The knit fabric was a bit clingy but not overly so, and there was a slit on the left side of the skirt, but it stopped at a very respectable point against her leg. Where did they come off saying such things?

"Well, she's going to make sure she wears something every day to catch the eye of all the male bosses," another woman, whose voice Adeline didn't recognize, spoke up. "Why else do you think she gets all those bonuses at the end of the year? I hear since she's come to work at Peak Experience Sports, she's slept with the majority of them."

Bonuses? Adeline had never received a bonus. As for sleeping with the male bosses, the mere idea made her sick to her stomach. Most of them were married with children.

Luella chuckled. "Everyone knows the Longsworths have money to burn. Makes you wonder why Adeline is working. For a paycheck?" Her chuckle was a sound of pure sarcasm. "I doubt it. I'm thinking she likes the extracurricular activity. You know what I mean?"

The women answered with spates of laughter, and Adeline struggled not to burst out of the bathroom stall and confront the whole miserable lot with the truth—they were classless, acid-tongued and an embarrassment to the female gender. But ultimately, what good would that do? Clearly, these women were not the gracious sort. They were jealous and hurtful. Even if she tried to defend herself with the truth, they wouldn't believe her. She'd only be giving them more gossip fodder. Besides, she wasn't about to give them the satisfaction of seeing the tears that were beginning to spill from her eyes.

Forcing herself not to move a muscle, Adeline remained in the stall and waited for what seemed like ages until the women left before she finally slipped out and hurried back to her desk.

By the time she reached her desk, her mind was made up. She wasn't going to continue to work in such a toxic environment. There had to be something better out there for her, and she was going to find it. With or without her parents' blessings.

After pulling her handbag from a locked drawer, she gathered up a gold ink pen and heart-shaped paperweight, tossed the items into the bag and switched off the computer.

As she headed out of the room, Brenda asked, "Going out?"

"Yes." *And I won't be back*, Adeline thought.

She walked out of the office and down the corridor to where a receptionist sat at a desk situated near the entrance of the building.

"I'm going out for lunch, Gwen."

The woman smiled and waved. "Have a nice one."

Too bad Louella and her cronies couldn't have been more like Gwen, Adeline thought. She was one of the few women in the building that she'd enjoyed knowing.

By the time she reached her little silver sports

car and climbed in the driver's seat, she felt resolute about her decision to leave Peak Experience Sports. Tomorrow, she'd let her boss know that it was impossible for her to return to work. To make up for not giving him a two-week notice, she'd tell him she'd forgo the wages owed her. It would be well worth every dollar, she thought grimly.

But that was tomorrow. Today, she was more concerned about finding Maddox John and learning whether his marriage proposal had been genuine, or if it was merely a pickup gimmick.

Later that afternoon, Maddox was up in the hayloft, taking inventory of the square bales used specifically for the ranch's remuda, when Pete, a longtime ranch hand for the Double J, called up to him.

"Hey, Maddox? You need to come down. There's someone here to see you."

Annoyed that Pete had interrupted his count, Maddox frowned and yelled down at him. "I'm not finished up here. Who is it?"

"Uh—don't ask questions, Maddox. Just get down here," he answered.

The insistent tone in Pete's voice made Maddox wonder if his father was behind Pete's summons. But on second thought, Randall wouldn't have Pete yelling up to the hayloft. He'd be doing it himself.

Curious now, Maddox walked over to an open square in the loft floor and climbed down the wooden ladder. He found Pete waiting for him at the bottom, and the ranch hand quickly jerked a thumb toward a spot behind him. Maddox looked beyond the cowboy's left shoulder and was instantly stunned to see Adeline Longsworth standing just inside the large double-door opening of the barn. And from the figure-hugging dress and pointed high heels she was wearing, she hadn't driven out here for a tour of the ranch.

"How long has she been here?" Maddox asked in a low voice.

"I don't know. I was riding up from the east pasture when I saw her getting out of her car." Pete whistled under his breath. "And let me tell you, Maddox, it's some car. One of those foreign sports jobs. Where did you meet her?"

"I'll, uh, tell you about it later," he said, then quickly strode past Pete and on to where Adeline was waiting.

As he drew near, she greeted him with a wide smile. "Hi, Maddox."

"Hello," he replied while thinking last night at DJ's Deluxe he'd made a terrible mistake. This woman wasn't merely beautiful; she was absolutely knockout gorgeous. "When Pete called me down from the loft, I certainly wasn't expecting to see you."

"Somehow I misplaced the number you gave me. Otherwise I would've called instead of just showing up out of the blue. Coming here to the ranch was the only way I could think of to contact you."

"Frankly, after I didn't hear from you, I decided you had torn up my number. After all, you did turn down my offer."

Her high cheekbones turned a soft pink color that made her face even more enchanting.

"That was last night," she replied. "And I've been doing some thinking. Is there somewhere we can go to talk? Or do you have time for me?"

For a second or two, Maddox wondered if he should pinch himself just to make sure he wasn't dreaming. Yes, this morning he'd been sure he would hear from her, but as time had marched on, he'd given up on the whole idea. The fact that she was here on the ranch was as jolting as the sight of a tornado racing across the plains.

Only this storm had warm brown eyes, soft pink lips and legs that went on forever. Normally, he would've considered Adeline to be perfect for fun dates and carefree romps in bed. But this wasn't dating, he reminded himself. Nor was it about a red-hot affair. This was about marriage and making everyone believe he was truly in love.

He didn't know how he was going to manage it, but if Adeline agreed to his proposal, he was going to have to fake his way through something he knew nothing about. And that something was being in love.

Chapter Three

Resting a hand against the small of her back, Maddox urged her out the door. "Let's get away from the barn," he said. "I don't want any of the hands to overhear us."

He guided her over to the shade tree with the octagon bench where, only this morning, he'd sat discussing his marriage plans with Wes. Never in Maddox's wildest imagination would he have guessed it would only be a matter of hours before Adeline would be sitting with him in the same spot.

"We could go in the house," he told her. "But considering the circumstances, I need to know what you're thinking before we see my family."

She nodded. "I totally agree. And sitting here is

fine," she said. "Actually, it's lovely here. The gold and orange leaves of this shade tree are beautiful. And the air is just cool enough to feel refreshing."

It was cool? She could've fooled him. Now that he was seated next to her, Maddox felt like it was the middle of July instead of the last part of September.

"I'm glad you're comfortable," he said, then glanced at his watch.

His father had left for Kalispell early this morning to meet with a cattle broker and then to price a few pieces of haying equipment. Maddox wasn't sure when Randall might get home, but he hoped it would be later rather than sooner. If his father drove up and caught Maddox sitting here with Adeline, he'd insist on meeting her. He'd also want to know what sort of relationship Maddox had with her. And that was something he and Adeline needed to iron out before they presented themselves to anyone as a couple.

"I'm sure you're wondering what I'm doing here," she said. "But like I told you a moment ago, I've been doing some thinking. And I need to know—were you serious last night about needing a wife?"

He looked at her, then drew in a deep breath. Something about the sound of the word *wife* on her lips rattled his train of thought.

"I was very serious. Did you think I was making everything up?"

She grimaced, then turned her gaze toward a ridge of mountains in the far distance. "I had just met you. I could hardly know what to think."

"You said you've been doing some thinking," he said guardedly. "About what?"

She squared her knees toward his so that she was facing him directly, and Maddox found it a struggle not to reach for her hands and draw her even closer.

"First of all, you should understand that I'm basically not an impulsive person," she said, "but today my behavior has—let's just say—veered from the norm. I quit my job."

A bit stunned, he stared at her. "Because of me? Because of my marriage offer?"

"No. You're not responsible. This is something I've been wanting to do for a long time, and today something happened that convinced me I couldn't go on working around people who consider me nothing more than rich trash."

He frowned with disbelief, and then as he caught a mixture of anger and sadness swirling in her eyes, he realized she was being truthful. "Sounds pretty cruel. Are you sure that's how they felt? Your coworkers said such things directly to your face?"

"No. Behind my back, but loud enough for me to hear." Shaking her head, she cast a rueful smile at him. "But that's done with. The second I walked out the door, I felt like I'd tossed away a heavy burden. And then suddenly I thought about your offer and how it would give me a chance to start my own business. Something I've wanted to do for a long time."

Maddox regarded her thoughtfully. "You'll probably consider my next question too personal, but I'm wondering why you would need money. Your family is obviously rich."

She drew in a deep breath and blew it out. "True. But my father is old school. He doesn't believe in just handing out money to his offspring. My younger sister and I will both have to prove to him that we're ready and able to handle a trust fund. As it stands, we won't get our allocations until we're thirty-five. I don't want to wait that long to step out on my own."

"Okay, I get that you don't want to wait. But if you wanted to be out on your own, I don't understand why you're still living on the Lazy L? Especially since you had a job that could've taken care of rent and that sort of thing."

She glanced away from him, but not before Maddox caught a glimpse of something akin to sadness in her eyes.

"Believe me, I've wondered the same thing. I guess—the main reason is that I've always loved the ranch. Living there was so nice until I grew up and Dad became so controlling. Then later on, well— each time I talked about moving out my mother would beg me to stay. She said she'd miss me too much if I left. And I suppose I used the excuse that she needed me to stay on the ranch. It was easier that way."

Strange, Maddox thought, but he did understand probably more than she realized. "And moving out on your own can be a bit scary. Especially when everything has always been provided for you."

"Dad has said I'm not mature enough to be on my own so many times that I think part of me had begun to believe him. But I'm finished with that," she said. "I do believe in myself and I do have the courage to stand on my own two feet."

Before he could stop himself Maddox asked, "So that's why you're here to see me? For the money?"

She turned a look of surprise on him. "What else? Money, or should I say wealth in a different form, is why you want to marry me. Right?"

Yes, he thought. He did want to marry her because of the Double J. And yet, it slapped his ego just a bit to hear her say she'd be marrying him for financial gain and nothing else.

Come on, Maddox! What's with the stupid, childish reaction? Emotions don't play into your game, remember? You're in this strictly for the profit.

Clearing his throat, he said in a brusque voice, "Right. It'll be nothing more than a business arrangement. Of course, there will be a few stipulations."

Her eyes narrowed skeptically. "What sort of stipulations?"

"Relax. I won't be demanding sex or anything of that nature. I only meant that when we're around family and friends, we must act as though we're madly in love with each other. Otherwise, everyone will see through the whole charade. If that happens, there's no way in hell Dad would change his will and sign over the major part of the ranch to me. Secondly, I think we'll need to stay married at least a year to get the legal end of the inheritance tied up neatly. After that happens, we can quietly divorce."

Her head swung back and forth as though he was relating a story too far-fetched to believe. "I do have a question about the inheritance. What's to stop your father from suddenly changing his mind and deciding he doesn't want to sign anything over to you?"

He chuckled softly. "You don't know Randall John. Once he makes a deal, he doesn't break it. Not for any reason. He's a man of his word."

"Okay, that's one concern out of the way. So what excuse are we going to use for divorcing after just a year? You snore? Or I smack when I chew my food? Maddox, I don't want to sound negative, but a divorce after twelve months is not going to look good for either of us, or our families."

"Well, we can stretch it out to fourteen or fifteen months if you think that will make the divorce seem more feasible. We can always use the standard reason—irreconcilable differences. And anyway, between now and then you might meet a guy you'll really want to marry."

She cocked a mocking brow at him. "How could that possibly happen? I don't believe we'd look very married if we started dating other people."

He realized he sounded like an idiot, but now—not after he'd slipped a ring on her finger—was the time to cover all the bases.

"Right. We can't date, obviously. But just in case you happen to look across the room and see a guy who makes your heart go thump, you'll know our setup is only temporary and you'll be free to find your true soul mate."

The wind was picking up strands of her long, dark brown hair and tossing them around her face. She tucked the wayward pieces behind her ear, and Maddox noticed, as he had last night, that her hands were slender, like the rest of her. He'd also noticed that her fingers were bare.

With her family's money, she could buy a jewelry box full of diamonds or other precious gems, he thought. But from what she'd just told him about her financial situation, she didn't want to depend on her family for money.

She wants to be independent, Maddox. It's important to her to have people see she can stand on her own without the help of her father. Just as you've felt ever since you were old enough to realize that you were viewed differently because of your family's wealth.

Her next question pushed away the little voice going off in his head.

"Well, have you stopped to think that it might be you who looks across the room and sees a woman that sends a thrill all the way to your toes?" She smiled wanly. "I hope that happens for you. For both of us. But in the meantime, I'm willing to give up a year or more to be able to start my own business."

"What sort of business?" he asked.

"A travel agency of my own."

He thought about that. "So, how much would you need to start your travel agency?"

She recited a number and his eyebrows raised. "I'm hardly an expert on the subject, but that sounds like a lot to start up a travel business."

Adeline shrugged. "Probably. But I'd need print and digital advertising. Because I'd have to compete heavily for clients. And then I would need to hire competent people who are good at the job and enjoyable to work with. All those things cost money."

He said, "I see. Well, I have money of my own. I can manage to pay you that much—once Dad changes his will and our marriage ends, of course. But I can't help wondering why you'd want to sink such a large amount of funds into a business of that sort."

She held up a hand as though to ward off his negative thoughts. "I know what you're going to say. With easy access to computers and the internet, people are booking their own travels and vacations. But there are plenty of people out there who don't have the time or the savvy to dig through the endless options offered on the web. It's much easier to tell an agent what you want and let that person do all the searching, booking, and confirming. Plus, an agent has the ability to locate special deals and bargains that aren't readily available to the general public. Along with procuring wedding venues and locations for special events."

"I hadn't thought about those angles," he said

thoughtfully. "So this is something you have your heart set on doing?"

Nodding eagerly, she said, "I realize I'm young and starting a business isn't easy, but I believe I can make it profitable. In spite of what Dad thinks."

"You've discussed such a venture with him?"

A tight grimace twisted her lips. "Certainly. I've asked him for a loan to begin building an agency, but he refuses. He gives me the same old excuses— I'm too immature and inexperienced to branch out on my own. He believes I should be satisfied at Peak Experience Sports taking orders from people who could care less about my future. For the past few years, I've worked my butt off for the company, but I was never once offered a promotion. I believe everyone has to pay their dues, but not to that extent."

She sounded resolute, and Maddox liked that about her. He figured once she made her mind up to do something, she couldn't be swayed.

"How do you think your parents are going to react about you quitting your job?"

"Very annoyed. Especially Dad. But if you and I get our plans cemented, then I'll have a good excuse to give my parents. I'll say I've met a man, one they'll definitely approve of, and that I wanted more time to invest in our relationship."

He gave her a clever grin. "Not a bad idea. Plant the notion in their minds so they won't be so shocked when we do announce our engagement."

Her delicate brows arched in question. "You plan on announcing our engagement soon?"

"Damn right! As soon as enough time passes for the whole thing to look credible. So let me go over the facts with you." He held up a hand and began ticking them off on his fingers. "You're going to get the big dream wedding you've always wanted. I'll draw up the agreement we've made in writing so we'll both feel confident that our business deal is what we agreed upon. And last but not least, the marriage will be in name only. Does that sound agreeable to you?"

"Yes," she answered, then frowned with doubt. "But how are we going to explain such a sudden, serious decision? No one knows that we've even met before, much less have had time to fall madly in love!"

The sound of an approaching vehicle had Maddox glancing over his shoulder, and he was relieved to see the truck didn't belong to his father but was one of the work trucks used by the ranch hands.

"Maddox, are you expecting someone?"

He looked at her. "Yes. Dad drove to Kalispell this morning, and I'm fairly sure he's going to drive up any minute."

"Oh, that might be awkward. Perhaps we should talk somewhere else?" she suggested. "Where he won't easily spot us?"

"No. The more I think about it, now might be a good time to let him find the two of us together.

The sooner we start this thing rolling, the better for us both."

She looked at him anxiously. "Don't we need to go over a few things first? Like how we met? How long we've been dating and things like that? I mean, he's bound to ask questions."

"Right. Let's walk over to the porch, and while we wait for him to show up, we'll go over our story."

With a hand resting casually against the small of her back, the two of them walked across the dusty stretch of ground from the ranch yard to the house.

Once they were on the porch, Maddox ushered her over to a love seat made of bent willow limbs and lined with soft red cushions. After she'd made herself comfortable, he sat down next to her, then purposely scooted near enough for their shoulders and thighs to touch.

The closeness caused her to direct a dry look at him. "Aren't you getting a little familiar?"

Her coolness put an amused grin on his face. "Don't worry. We need the practice."

"What we need is an explanation for all of this," she primly reminded him.

"Oh yes, explanations," he repeated. "Let me think. We need to put together a sensible scenario. One that will satisfy not only our parents but the rest of our family and friends."

"Precisely," she replied. "And I'm not very good at making up stories."

He very nearly laughed but managed to stifle the

urge. Now wasn't the time to offend her. "You mean you're basically not a good liar?"

"No. Even as a child, if I tried to tell a fib, my parents or sister could usually see through me."

He groaned. "Oh man. Well, you're going to have to practice up on the fibbing, because we're going to have to do plenty of skirting around the truth."

"I'm sure you won't. Have to practice, that is," she said knowingly. "I imagine you've made deception an art form."

He slapped a hand over the region of his heart. "That's tough, Adeline."

She rolled her eyes. "Unfortunately, your experience at subterfuge is needed now."

Did she think he purposely went around lying to women, or his family? He could understand why she'd have the idea, but he didn't like it. Maddox had never made a habit of trying to mislead anyone. Especially the women he'd dated. False promises weren't his style.

But he couldn't waste time trying to defend his character now, Maddox thought. And anyway, Adeline's opinion of him shouldn't matter. He needed a wife, and if she considered him a heel, that was her problem, not his.

He drew in a deep breath and blew it out. "Okay. Since no one has seen us together—except your friend last night—I think we'll have to say that we've been seeing each other in secret for a few weeks."

From her expression, she considered his idea

worse than far-fetched. "I hope you have a good reason for the secrecy. Otherwise, we're both going to look stupid."

"True. So give me a moment to think." A myriad of options clicked through his mind until it stopped on an idea that felt more feasible to him than anything else. He snapped his fingers and said, "Our fathers had a feud, right? And knowing my father, I'm sure he had plenty of derogatory things to say about your father. Although, I honestly don't remember the feud. Dad has had too many disputes with people over the years to single out just one. But anyway, you and I feared our families wouldn't approve of us dating, so we kept it quiet. But now we've had enough time to realize we love each other and want to get married soon, so we could no longer keep quiet about our feelings."

She tilted her head to one side and regarded him thoughtfully. "Makes sense. Sort of."

Annoyed that she wasn't praising him for the idea, especially after he'd come up with it on the spur of the moment, he asked, "You have a better suggestion?"

"Not really," she admitted. "I only wish we had something more concrete."

He shrugged. "This is as about as concrete as we're going to get. Besides, from what I've seen of my friends and family, people don't act rationally when they're in love. And we are supposed to be besotted with each other. Hopefully, everyone will think we were in a dreamy fog and weren't using good judgment about keeping everything a secret."

Unimpressed, she said, "You don't exactly sound like a man who views marriage in a good light."

He grimaced. "Sorry. It's not on my to-do list. I've seen too many bad outcomes with engagements and marriages. Anyway, I relish my freedom. Don't you?"

"Depends on how you interpret freedom," she answered sagely. "I happen to think that loving someone—really loving—doesn't mean being trapped or boxed in. It means a lifetime of sharing and supporting each other."

Oh, Lord, he should have guessed she held a syrupy-sweet idea about love and marriage. Having a husband and children had probably been a dream of hers since her childhood days. Thankfully, though, she currently appeared to be more focused on building a business for herself than starting a family. In any case, Maddox wasn't worried she'd get any clingy ideas toward him. He'd already made it clear that theirs would be a platonic merger, and he'd have the stipulation plainly written in their contract.

"When did you start wearing rose-colored glasses?" he asked bluntly. "Or have they always been your choice of eyewear?"

She shot him a smirk. "Nothing wrong with my eyes, but have you thought about getting yours checked? I'm beginning to think your field of vision is far too narrow."

He chuckled. "Could be just the opposite. I might see too much."

"Well, before we *see* your dad driving up, or your mom walks out of the house and finds us here on the porch, we should probably go over a few details. If we've been dating for weeks, we should at least know the names of our future in-laws and a little personal information about each other."

Nodding in agreement, he said, "Right. And we don't have much time. You go first, and then I'll tell you all about myself."

With a condescending smile, she reached over and placed her hand over the top of his. "I imagine you have a much longer history than I do, Maddox. You better go first."

The touch of her hand sent warm tremors up his arm and, unable to stop it, his gaze fixed on the moist curve of her lips.

Damn. Being this woman's husband was going to be a challenge in more ways than one, he decided.

But then, nothing good ever came from taking the easy way.

A little more than a half hour later, a cloud of dust rose from the ranch yard as Randall John braked his truck to a stop and promptly stepped out. As Adeline watched the John patriarch take long, quick strides toward the house, she felt as though she'd just taken a crash course on Maddox and his family's life. Her mind was buzzing with names, places, hobbies,

work and countless other bits of information, and
she feared that once she was standing face-to-face
with the wizened rancher, she wouldn't remember
a single fact.

Next to her, Maddox bent his head and whispered
close to her ear. "Dad will be on the porch in just a
few seconds. So this will be our first test. Just put
a dreamy smile on your face and let me do most of
the talking."

"I'll do my best to be convincing," she promised
while asking herself what the heck she was getting
into. She'd been honest with Maddox when she'd
told him she wasn't normally an impulsive person.
So how did she rationalize going from her humdrum
daily schedule to this subterfuge of love with Maddox John? Had she gone a bit crazy? Or had she simply broken out of the protective shell her parents had
attempted to keep around her?

Just as Randall was climbing the steps, Maddox
clasped her hand and drew the both of them to a
standing position.

"Don't act surprised," he whispered. "We need to
start practicing now. So let's give him a good first
image—that we're crazy in love."

Before Adeline could ask what sort of practicing
he was talking about, he pulled her into his arms and
planted his lips over hers.

The intimate contact shocked her to the point that
all she could do was stand stock-still in the circle of

his arms and allow his lips to make a slow, heated search of hers.

And then suddenly every cell in her body burst to life and buzzed with sensations she'd never experienced. Kissing Maddox was like the unfolding layers of a dark mystery, with each one more thrilling than the last. At some point during their stunning lip-lock, Adeline forgot all about acting. Her arms unwittingly curled around his neck, and her body snuggled up to his.

It wasn't until she heard Randall John loudly clearing his throat that she regained her senses enough to step back from Maddox's embrace.

"Maddox, is this some new form of ranch work?" his father asked.

Her cheeks burning, Adeline dared to glanced at Maddox, and the cagey grin on his face made her wonder if he'd been feeling the same zingers she'd been experiencing. Or was she alone in feeling like she'd just downed a stiff cocktail?

Maddox curved a possessive arm around Adeline's shoulders as he turned the both of them toward his father. "Better than roping and branding," he said to Randall. "Dad, I want you to meet Adeline. I guess the cat is out of the bag. You saw for yourself how we feel about each other."

Randall's keen gaze traveled over Maddox, then moved on to Adeline. "It looked like mutual affection to me," he said, then offered his hand to Adeline. "A pleasure to meet you, young lady. Have you known my son long enough to figure out he's a rascal?"

The lump of nerves in her throat made it difficult to form a word, but somehow she managed to give the tall, dark-haired rancher the dreamy smile that Maddox had talked about earlier. "Well, we've known each other long enough for me to know he's a pretty wonderful guy."

Randall was clearly bemused by Adeline's remark, which made her wonder just exactly what sort of women Maddox had presented to his parents in the past.

Maddox quickly stepped in. "Dad, I apologize for not bringing Adeline around sooner to meet you and Mom. We—uh—have been dating steadily for quite a while now but haven't told anybody about it until today. We—"

"Maddox, you should be ashamed of yourself!" Randall interrupted in a playful tone. "Why would you be hiding a beautiful woman like Adeline?"

"I haven't been hiding her," Maddox informed him. "I— We thought— Well, we weren't quite sure how you, especially, would accept her. See, Adeline is a Longsworth. Louis Longsworth is her father."

Pushing back the brim of his black cowboy hat, Randall arched his brows as he studied the both of them. "So I'm guessing you finally decided I'm not a man to hold grudges?"

The faint tug at the corners of Maddox's lips made Adeline fear he was on the verge of bursting out with laughter. But just as quickly the look of amusement turned to one of gravity.

"We were hoping that would be the case, Dad. Because I love Adeline." He reached for her hand and clasped it tightly between both of his. "And we plan to be together—for always."

If Randall was surprised to hear Maddox's declaration, he didn't show it. Instead, he studied the two of them for what seemed like an eternity to Adeline.

Finally he asked, "Have you spoken to your mother about this yet?"

"No. We've been waiting on you to get home," Maddox told him.

"She'll be wanting to meet Adeline. Let's go in and find her." Randall looked over at Adeline and winked. "Mimi promised to bake me a pumpkin pie for dessert—one of the best things about autumn. And Maddox can tell you that his mother's pies are the best. You will stay for supper, won't you?"

Considering the circumstances of the land grant, Adeline had never expected Randall John to be so friendly toward her. And his warm invitation caught her totally off guard.

"Oh, I don't know," she hedged as she darted a questioning look at Maddox. "I wouldn't want to be a bother and cause Mrs. John extra cooking."

Maddox curled an arm around her waist and smiled adoringly down at her. Adeline could only wonder if this was the type of look he gave all his women. No. It was an act, she told herself. Just like that kiss he'd plastered on her lips.

"Of course she's going to stay, Dad," Maddox told him. "We've been looking forward to having dinner with you."

Randall slapped an affectionate hand on his son's shoulder. "Great. Let's go in and find your mother."

"I imagine she's in the kitchen," Maddox told him as they entered the house.

Randall laughed. "She'd better be," he said, then cast Adeline another wink. "Just kidding, Adeline. If my wife spends a lot of her time in the kitchen, it's because she wants to be there. Not because I demand it."

She smiled at him. "I never thought that for a minute, Mr. John. If you're anything like Maddox, I'm positive you treat your wife like a queen."

From the corner of her eye, she saw a faint arch to Maddox's brows. Apparently, her compliment had surprised him. Especially after he'd told her to let him do all the talking. But she figured it was best that he learned from the start that she wasn't a meek little female he could order about.

"Now, none of this *Mr. John* stuff, Adeline. Call me Randall," he said with a wide smile, then slanted a pointed look at his son. "Maddox, I'm already liking your young lady. If you have any sense at all, you won't let her get away."

Wow! Adeline hadn't expected things to go this easily. However, she needed to remember this was only the beginning. There was no way of knowing what sort of obstacles the two of them were going to encounter on their way to becoming engaged, much less getting married.

"Dad, letting Adeline get away is the one thing I never intend to do," Maddox assured his father.

Until a year or so passes and Randall signs over the major part of the Double J to Maddox. As the thought raced through Adeline's mind, why was it followed by a trail of sadness?

Chapter Four

Later that night, after a first-rate meal of rib eye steak, scalloped potatoes, snow peas, tossed green salad and the promised pumpkin pie, Randall suggested they take their coffee into the den.

Part of Maddox wanted to make excuses for him and Adeline to end the evening with his parents. Especially when Adeline was probably exhausted from staying constantly on guard during dinner. Randall and Mimi had bombarded her with all sort of questions. Most had been mundane, but some had been pertinent and tricky. Yet Adeline had maneuvered through them as if she'd known Maddox for months rather than mere hours. Not only that, she'd managed to charm both his parents while dodging the bullets.

Now, as Maddox sat close to Adeline on a couch angled in front of a crackling fire his father had built in the fireplace only minutes earlier, he wondered how he'd managed to get so lucky. Over the years, he'd been in the bar at DJ's Deluxe too many times to count, and he'd never once caught a glimpse of Adeline Longsworth. Then, just when he needed the right woman to come into his life, he looked around and there she sat, like an exotic flower just waiting for him to pick. With that kind of luck, Maddox ought to be in Vegas.

Mimi said, "It was only a few days ago I was talking with some of my friends in town about all the recent engagements and marriages in Bronco. I told them how I'd dreamed about Maddox bringing a special girl home to meet his parents." She laughed with delight as she placed her coffee cup on an end table wedged between her wing chair and Randall's big leather recliner. "I honestly didn't know my dream was going to come true. And so soon, at that!"

Maddox slipped his arm across Adeline's shoulders and hugged her a fraction closer to his side. He didn't know what exactly it was about her—maybe it had something to do with her soft skin or the flowery scent swirling about her, but touching her was different, somehow. Just having his fingers resting on her upper arm filled him with a pleasure that was downright silly. He wasn't a randy teenager dreaming of having sex for the first time. He was an experienced thirty-year-old man who'd had an array of women in his arms. This one wasn't different, he promised himself—she only felt that way.

"You didn't tell me about this dream, Mom," he said. "I would've enjoyed hearing it."

Mimi rolled her eyes. "So you could laugh at me? You've always dated lots of women, Maddox. Your father and I never dreamed you were getting serious about anyone. You never gave us a clue."

Adeline glanced at him, then smiled at his mother. "Please don't blame Maddox for keeping secrets, because it's really all my fault, Mimi. I was worried you and your husband would resent me—for being a Longsworth, that is."

Most folks around Bronco considered Randall the tough backbone of the Johns, but Maddox could tell them they had it all wrong. Mimi had always been the firm foundation of the family. True, when it came to making business decisions for the ranch, she was content to let her husband call the shots. But when it came to her family's personal welfare, that was a different matter. Her word ruled, and no one, including Randall, could change her mind.

Mimi batted a dismissive hand through the air. "You were worrying for nothing. That old feud has long been forgotten. Isn't that right, honey?"

She looked over at her husband, and Randall nodded in agreement.

"When one door closes, another one opens. After the grant went to your father," Randall said to Adeline, "a large section of grazing land came up for sale, and I managed to snare it. The property is even better than what Louis and I were fighting over, so I came out the winner."

Coming out the winner was important to his father, Maddox thought. Randall liked to win, and he liked to impress. That's why he and Mimi were longing to see one of their children exchange wedding vows in front of half the county. Silly or not, Maddox could understand a bit of his father's feelings. Every man had his pride. Some of them just took it to a higher degree.

"I'm very happy to hear there are no hard feelings," Adeline told him.

Randall looked at her. "How does Louis feel about you and Maddox? I hope he isn't harboring a grudge against us Johns. I'd hate for you and Maddox to have to deal with that sort of headache."

Maddox could feel Adeline's shoulders stiffen slightly, and he hastened to alleviate her unease. "Don't worry, Dad. We're not fretting about Adeline's father."

Adeline cleared her throat. "Actually, I haven't told my parents about Maddox yet. We wanted to give you two the news first. I plan to talk with my family tonight or tomorrow."

Randall's eyes narrowed, while Mimi grimaced, but thankfully neither of his parents commented on Adeline's revelation. And if they thought the whole thing strange, neither said as much. Maddox was thrilled that this initial introduction of Adeline to his parents had gone off without a hitch. Not only that, they seemed happier with the unexpected news than he could have ever hoped them to be. It almost made him feel guilty. But only almost.

Another hour passed with the four of them making small talk. Adeline made no glaring mistakes in her remarks, and neither did Maddox. Then Adeline announced she needed to head back to her home, which was a substantial drive from the Double J.

Before they left the house, Mimi gave Adeline an affectionate hug and kiss on the cheek while Randall shook her hand and made her promise to come again soon.

"Don't worry, Dad," Maddox told him, "you're going to be seeing a lot of Adeline around here."

"Good to hear," he said to his son, then turned to Adeline. "I'm sorry Charity was out with friends tonight and didn't get to meet you. She's going to be thrilled to have a woman closer to her age visiting the ranch."

"I'm looking forward to meeting your daughter," Adeline said. "And to seeing both of you again. Thank you for the lovely dinner. After eating your cooking, Mimi, I think you need to give me a few lessons in the kitchen."

Mimi beamed with pleasure. "I'll be glad to give you cooking pointers. But I have the feeling Maddox doesn't care whether you can cook or not."

Maddox chuckled, but inwardly he wondered if his mother would understand or ever forgive him if she discovered the truth. Mimi was like most mothers. She was eager for her children to be happily married and making babies. She would be highly disappointed whenever he and Adeline divorced.

Hell, Maddox, you're not even married to the woman yet and you're already worrying about getting a divorce. You can't start feeling guilty or sentimental now!

Trying to ignore the taunting voice in his head, he smiled at his mother. "You're right, Mom. Adeline doesn't need to cook to make me happy."

Randall laughed, and after exchanging a few more teasing remarks, he and Mimi happily waved them off.

Inside the foyer, Maddox grabbed a jean jacket from a hall tree by the door and draped it around Adeline's shoulders. "You don't have a coat with you," he explained when she darted him a look of surprise. "The night air will be cold."

"Thanks. But what about yourself?" she asked as she eyed his denim shirt. "You might need a jacket, too."

With her next to him? No. He'd never feel the cold, Maddox thought.

"I'll be fine," he assured her.

The two of them left the house, and as they headed across the hard-packed ground of the ranch yard to where Adeline had parked her car, Maddox suddenly stopped and, turning his face skyward, let out loud howl.

Adeline stared at him. "What is that supposed to be? You sounded like a dog in pain!"

Laughing, he said, "Wrong. That's a happy coyote who's just found his mate."

Her lips took on a dry slant. "You're familiar with that sound, are you?"

"Sure. Small packs of the animals run here on the ranch. Most nights you can hear them howling over in the foothills. Did you know a coyote mates for life? No fooling around for those canines. They stick it out till death do them part."

Her expression said she didn't believe anything he said. And Maddox supposed he couldn't blame her. So far their whole relationship was based on make-believe.

She asked mockingly, "What if they encounter irreconcilable differences between them? They go to coyote court for a divorce?"

Wrapping his arm around her shoulders, he made a tsking noise with his tongue. "Oh, my little jaded sweetheart, I'm telling you the truth—about the coyotes."

"Hmm. Well, you and I aren't going to be like a coyote couple. We'll be splitting once this farce has ended. You—"

"Quiet!" Maddox shushed her as he spotted a male figure striding out of the shadows and straight toward them. "Here comes my big brother. He's the last person I want to find out about our plan."

Unlike Maddox and Dawson, who still lived in the

main ranch house with the rest of the family, Jameson had his own house situated on a hill a short distance up from the main ranch house. He was already firmly ensconced on the Double J and held no worries that he would one day reign over the ranch and his two younger brothers. But Maddox had news for Jameson. This wasn't a monarchy. He wasn't about to stand by and allow Jameson to take control of the land and livestock. Ever since Maddox was a young boy, barely able to throw a leg over the saddle, the ranch had been firmly entrenched in his heart, and he was just as deserving of the Double J as anyone.

"Jameson," Maddox greeted his brother. "I'm glad you showed up just now. I want you to meet my special girl—Adeline Longsworth."

Jameson's stunned gaze whipped back and forth between Maddox and Adeline until he finally stepped forward and extended a hand to her.

"Nice to meet you, Adeline," he said. "I'm Maddox's older brother. Just in case he hasn't told you."

Smiling, she politely shook his hand. "Oh yes, Maddox has told me all about you and his other siblings. It's a pleasure to meet you, Jameson."

"Adeline and I just had dinner with the folks," Maddox gleefully informed him. "Rib eyes. You should've showed up. The meal was great."

Jameson's eyes narrowed with speculation, and Maddox figured his head had to be spinning. As far as his older brother knew, Maddox had never planned on having, or wanting, a special girl. No doubt seeing Adeline here on the ranch and hearing she'd had dinner with their parents was a shocker to him.

The idea had Maddox chuckling to himself. It would do his brother good to do a bit of squirming, he thought.

"I had some chores to tend," Jameson told him.

Maddox looked past his brother's shoulder to where he'd parked his truck next to their father's. "Vanessa isn't with you?"

"No. Vanessa had something to do in town this evening."

"That's too bad. Adeline is looking forward to meeting her."

"I'll be sure and let her know," Jameson said, then turned his full attention to Adeline. "The name Longsworth sounds familiar. Do you live in the area?"

"Yes. My parents, Louis and Naomi, own the Lazy L. I live on the ranch with them. It's about a half hour drive from here."

Jameson nodded, then darted Maddox a sly look. "Sure. The Lazy L. If I recall, Louis Longsworth won the land grant Dad wanted."

Adeline's smile never wavered, and Maddox found his respect for her growing by the minute.

"You're exactly right," she told him. "But thankfully your wonderful father has put that uncomfortable incident in the past. I hope you can, too, Mr. John. Because I'm sure I'll be seeing more of you and your family in the coming weeks."

He noticed Jameson's brows inching up ever so slightly. No doubt Adeline's suggestion had sent his mind spinning even faster, and the idea left Maddox struggling to keep from laughing out loud. Woo-hoo! This was getting to be too much fun, he thought.

"Call me Jameson," he told her. "And I'm happy to hear we'll be seeing more of you. I've been telling Maddox for some time that he needs to find himself someone special."

Maddox hugged Adeline closer to his side. "See, brother, I take more of your good advice than you think I do."

Jameson purposely cleared his throat. "Well, I'll let you two be on your way. I need to talk with Dad about a few things."

"Your wedding?" Maddox asked out of curiosity. If for some reason Jameson and Vanessa did decide to relent and go for an outlandish wedding to please their parents, then this ruse he and Adeline had started would all be for naught.

Jameson frowned. "No. Dad isn't about to influence our wedding plans. This is about bulls and heifers. Want to join in?"

Maddox was relieved but did his best not to show it. "Maybe later," he told him. "I want to see Adeline off first."

Jameson nodded, then smiled politely at Adeline. "A pleasure to meet you, Adeline. I'm getting the feeling that you're just what my little brother needs."

"That's funny," Maddox said. "Before dinner, Dad basically said the same thing to me."

"Like father, like son. You two have a good evening." He lifted a hand in farewell, then strode off toward the house.

Once Jameson was out of earshot, Adeline let out a long, pent-up breath. "Oh, I'm not sure about him, Maddox. I had the feeling he was seeing straight through us."

Maddox gave her cheek an encouraging pat. "Don't worry. You were great. Yeah, right about now Jameson is probably suspicious of the two of us. But he'll come around. Once he sees us together for a while."

"Yes, but will he think our romance is fabricated just to win your father's favor? The inheritance?"

"Maybe. But Jameson can't prove it," Maddox assured her. "There's no way he or any of our family members can actually know how the two of us feel about each other. Unless we accidently slip and say something in front of them. And I don't think either of us is stupid enough to let our guard down, do you?"

She rolled her eyes. "I'm beginning to wonder if we're both idiots to think we can pull this off."

With a hand against her back, he urged her forward. "It's cold out here and you're beginning to shiver. Let's finish our talk in your car."

When they reached the silver sports car, he helped her into the driver's seat, and while she started the engine and turned on the heater, he made himself comfortable in the passenger seat.

She squared her knees toward the console in order to face him directly and through the semidarkness of the car's interior, Maddox could see her expression was strained.

Wanting to allay her doubts, he gathered her hand in his and gave it an encouraging squeeze.

"Okay. You're beginning to wonder if we're both idiots. But you're wrong, Adeline. We can pull this thing off. We have the worst behind us already. At least as far as my family is concerned. Now, if I can manage to win over your parents, we'll begin convincing everyone else around here."

"My parents," she ruefully repeated. "They'll be a real test—for both of us."

Undeterred, he grinned. "I've always been pretty good at tests. So how do you want to work this? I can drive over to the Lazy L most anytime this week and meet them."

She looked aghast. "No! Not yet!" she burst out, then, seeing his puzzled expression, quickly attempted to explain. "I—uh—I mean Dad is very, very protective of his two daughters. Especially when it comes to men. I'm sure the situation will be less of a problem if I break the news to him and Mom before you actually show up."

He frowned. "Sounds as though you believe he's going to give us a problem about getting married."

She looked completely bemused and then suddenly she covered her face with her hands and began to laugh. "Us getting married! This is a riot! It's hilarious!"

Maddox let her go on with the laughter until the sound took on a tortured tone, and then he reached for her shoulders.

"Aw, honey, it's all going to work. Right now your nerves are jangled." He pulled her head against his shoulder and gently stroked her back. "You've done a heck of a job tonight. Especially since you only had a few minutes to get prepared for all this. I'm impressed."

She sniffed and pulled her head back just enough to look at his face. Maddox was instantly aware of the closeness of her lips and her soft breath fanning his cheeks.

"Really?" she asked.

He smiled at her while telling himself he didn't actually want to kiss her. Whether her lips would taste as sweet as they had when he'd kissed her on the porch was a question he didn't need to answer.

He said, "You've handled all of this like a champ."

"So why do I feel as low as a snake?" she asked. "I'll tell you, Maddox, I didn't like fibbing to your parents. They were so nice and accepting of me. And I—I'm nothing but a fake! Don't you feel awful about it?"

Shaking his head, he let out a long breath. "Okay, maybe I do. Just a little. On the other hand, I realize that you and I will eventually be giving my parents their greatest wish—a chance to give one of their children an elaborate, over-the-top wedding. Ultimately, we'll be making them happy. That should be your main focus."

A doubtful expression turned down the corners of her lips. "Well, yes. We'll be making them happy for a little while. Until we divorce."

He let out a tired groan. "Don't dwell on that part of the deal, Adeline. Even couples who begin their marriage madly in love can't predict the long-term outcome. Who knows, a deadly accident or disease could take one of us out before a divorce happens. Life is a gamble—an uncertainty. Which is a good reason for us to grab all the joy and profit we can when it's offered to us."

She closed her eyes and drew in a deep breath. "In other words, go for the gusto and don't worry about the consequences."

The nearby glow of a yard lamp filtered enough light into the car to illuminate her face. Maddox found himself studying the way her black lashes created dark crescents against her pale skin, and he noticed the slight quiver at the corners of her lips. She looked so lovely and vulnerable, he thought. And before he could stop himself, Maddox gently cupped her cheek.

"I'm not heartless, Adeline. I do think about the future. That's what this is all about. My future and yours. In the end, we're not going to hurt anyone. If we see we're causing anyone true misery, then we'll call the whole thing off."

She opened her eyes, and as Maddox gazed into the warm brown depths, he felt an icy prick at the back of his neck. He'd never planned to have such a visceral reaction to this woman. He wasn't supposed to care what she was thinking or feeling. His only concern should be whether she was playing the character of his loving partner in convincing fashion. Yet, Maddox realized he didn't want her to be sad, or hurt, or disillusioned with him. And that could turn him into the worst kind of fool.

"You'd really do that?" she asked.

Would he? Maddox wanted to think he was a man of honor. But if push came to shove, was he honorable enough to step aside and lose the majority share of his beloved home? Damn it, he had to believe he would. And Adeline had to believe it, too.

"Yes. I'd really do that," he murmured. "Trust me?"

Uncertainty flickered in her eyes. "I want to get out from under my father's thumb. I want to stand on my own—do and be what I want rather than what he believes I should be—just a dutiful daughter who depends on him until she marries a man who gets his approval. So you see, if this ruse of a marriage will help me accomplish that goal, then I'll have to trust you."

He wished he could've heard a bit more resolution

in her voice, but for now he had to be satisfied with the fact that she seemed to want to stick to the plan.

"Good," he murmured, then, clearing his throat, he forced himself to ease her out of his arms. "So now we need to get to work. Will you be available to go to dinner with me tomorrow night? I think the sooner people start seeing us together, the more likely they'll believe our engagement."

Frowning thoughtfully, she said, "Right off the top of my head, I can't think of any reason why I can't meet you for dinner."

"Great. I'll see if I can get reservations at DJ's Deluxe. Hopefully some of my Bronco Heights acquaintances will be there."

Her brows arched in a speculative way. "What about Bronco Valley? Do you have acquaintances from there?"

Bronco was separated into two sections. Bronco Heights was the portion of town where the upper crust resided. Bronco Valley was more of a blue-collar area.

"Sure. I've always had friends from all walks of life. My parents might enjoy displaying their wealth, but deep down, they aren't snobs. What about you? Do you ever rub elbows in Bronco Valley?"

Her expression was suddenly sheepish. "Uh, not exactly. Frankly, my parents are snobs, and they've tried to raise me and Emily in their image. You know—picking and screening our friends and the people we associate with."

"You're a grown woman. Surely you can pick your own friends now."

She let out a short, caustic laugh. "Oh, yes, I can. But they might not end up being my friend for long. Remember Spence? In my parents' eyes, he wasn't good enough, so he conveniently disappeared. They have ways of eliminating anyone who doesn't measure up."

"I can see why you want to stand on your own. I couldn't take that sort of controlling." He gave her a mischievous grin. "But I'm going to get you away from their grip and show you how the lower-class parties in Bronco Valley."

Smiling now, she squared back around in the seat and snapped her seat belt in place. "I imagine you've partied with the best of both worlds."

He chuckled. "It pays to be well-rounded, Adeline."

She started to reach for the gearshift, then paused. "Oh, I almost forgot. You need your jacket back."

He wrapped a hand over her forearm, preventing her from removing the seat belt and his jacket. "Keep the jacket," he insisted. "It'll give you a good reason to come back to the ranch."

"All right." She gave him a little smile that was impossible to decipher. "Good night, Maddox."

"Good night, Adeline. Drive carefully."

He lifted a hand in farewell, then hurriedly climbed out of the car before he changed his mind and gave her a real kiss.

Chapter Five

"You can't be serious, Adeline! You can't just quit your job on the spur of the moment!"

Adeline took a sip of coffee from the cup her mother had kindly brought to her bedroom. After the chaotic day yesterday and the long drive home from the Double J last night, she'd slept much later than she'd planned.

"I can and I have," she said.

Less than two minutes had passed since Naomi had knocked on her daughter's door to find out why she wasn't already up and readying herself for work. Now that Adeline had informed her that she no longer worked for Peak Experience Sports, her mother still refused to believe it.

"But, Adeline! After all the effort your father made to get you that job. He—"

From her seat on the edge of the bed, Adeline held up a hand to halt her mother's coming lecture. "Yes, Mom, you don't have to remind me. Dad got me the job. I didn't get it on my own merit. But that's only because I didn't want it in the first place. I had no desire to work for that company, and frankly, I want to kick up my heels at the fact I'll never have to step foot in the building again."

Naomi stood in the middle of the room, wringing her hands and staring at Adeline as if she'd suddenly turned into a stranger. And as Adeline studied her mother, she couldn't help but notice the differences in her and Maddox's mother, Mimi.

At fifty-one, Naomi was still a young woman, and for the most part she looked it, with her reddish-brown hair cut in a youthful bob and her tall figure carrying exactly the right amount of weight. Of course, she worked at looking her best, Adeline thought, but being wealthy made the task easier. Naomi could frequent the best spas and salons, treat her complexion to expensive skin care, and have the healthiest food at her fingertips. She'd lived a pampered life as a child, and it had continued on after she'd married Louis.

As for Mimi, Maddox's mother was equally well-preserved and lovely in appearance. Especially considering the fact that she'd raised three strapping sons and a daughter. But there was a softness about Mimi, a down-to-earth quality about her that set her apart from Naomi and made Adeline wish that whenever she got married for real, she'd be lucky enough to have a mother-in-law like her.

"Adeline! What has come over you? I've never heard you talk so disrespectfully before."

Adeline looked down at the coffee in her cup while thinking she'd like to say a whole lot more. Like how she knew her parents had bullied Spence out of her life. But she forced the bitter words to remain on her tongue. She couldn't be giving her parents or anyone the impression that she was still pining over Spence. She had to somehow make everyone believe she'd been falling in love with Maddox all this time.

Sighing, Adeline rose from the bed and reached for the satin robe lying across a dressing bench. "I'm not being disrespectful, Mom. I'm being honest. And you know it."

Behind her, she heard Naomi's short gasp and knew if she glanced over her shoulder, she'd see a shocked look on her mother's face.

"Well, let's not split hairs over how you got the job, Adeline. The fact is that you need it. What is your boss going to think? You're going to have to come up with some important excuse for leaving yesterday and not showing up this morning. I—"

"Forget it, Mom. I'm not making excuses. I'm calling Mr. Miller in a few minutes and letting him know I won't be back. That's final," she added firmly.

There was a long pause, and then Naomi said, "Okay. I can see you've made up your mind. But I think I deserve to know what brought all of this about. Your father is certainly going to want an explanation for this sudden change in you!"

Adeline knotted the sash of the robe at her waist, then turned to face her mother. "Actually, I do have an explanation. A wonderful one, at that."

Naomi's blue eyes narrowed with wary anticipation. "Oh? And what are you calling wonderful?"

"I—uh—haven't mentioned this before now, but seeing that my life is about to change, it's time I told you and Dad. A special man has come into my life, and though I plan to get another job eventually, I'm going to be giving him most of my attention."

The news apparently took more out of her mother than Adeline had expected it to. She sank onto the dressing bench at the foot of the bed and pressed a palm against her forehead.

"A man! I—I'm not understanding this, Adeline. You told me not long ago that Spence left—that he moved to another town. Don't tell me he's returned!"

Any other time, Adeline's teeth would have been snapping together with anger. Just to hear her mother act so innocently ignorant about Spence's departure was not only cruel, it was insulting. But amazingly, Adeline realized she didn't care if Spence had flown to the other side of the world, or even the moon. And as for Naomi and Louis's clandestine interference in their daughter's love life, well, Adeline was about to make them wish they'd left her innocuous boyfriend alone.

"Mom, I'm not talking about Spence." To emphasize her words, she added a little laugh. "He was mostly just a friend I enjoyed going around with. This man is—well, I love him, deeply. Seriously."

Naomi was astonished. "But how has this happened? When did you meet him?"

Adeline walked over to the large bay window that gave her a splendid view of the distant mountains. The hardwoods growing along the foothills were turning vibrant shades of gold and red, while on the highest peaks, small patches of white snow were beginning to form.

Mimi promised to bake me a pumpkin pie—one of the best things about autumn. She remembered Randall John's words.

Funny, but Adeline couldn't ever recall her mother making special desserts for her father. She showed her love by making sure Louis remained on a diet low in fat and sugar. And to a certain extent that was good, Adeline supposed. But once in a while, life should include enjoying simple pleasures.

Turning, she gave her mother the happiest smile she could conjure up. "I met him this past summer in Bronco—during the Fourth of July festivities. Since then our feelings have steadily grown into love."

Naomi's nostrils flared with disapproval, which hardly surprised Adeline. Her parents disliked either of their daughters doing anything without their consent first. No matter that Adeline was now twenty-five and Emily twenty-one. In her parents' eyes, they weren't mature enough to live without constant guidance. Actually, it was a miracle they'd allowed Emily to go off to college in Billings. But because she'd won a full scholarship, they'd been forced to give in to save face with their friends.

"And who is this young man you've fallen so deeply in love with? Do your father and I know him?"

Adeline couldn't start wavering now, she thought. Maddox needed her to carry this through. Just as much as she needed him to get her out of this claw hold on her life.

"I doubt you've ever met him personally. But yes, you've heard of his family—the Johns. He's Maddox John. Randall and Mimi's second-oldest son."

Naomi's mouth formed a perfect O. "You mean the Johns who stabbed your father in the back by trying to sneak the land grant away from him?"

Adeline inwardly groaned. She was sick of hearing about her father's land-grabbing, moneymaking ways. Yes, his wealth had allowed Adeline to grow up in luxury, but that didn't mean she was always proud of his tactics.

"Mom, that was over with long ago. The Johns certainly aren't dwelling on the matter."

Naomi sniffed. "Well, of course the Johns wouldn't want to dwell on the issue. They lost."

Rolling her eyes, Adeline walked over to the

closet and began to riffle through the array of designer dresses she allotted for parties and nights on the town. With tonight being her and Maddox's first real date—well, sort of real—she wanted to make sure she made a good impression on anyone who might see them together.

"I shouldn't have to warn you, Adeline, that your father isn't going to be pleased with this news. Especially that you've taken up with a John."

Struggling to hold on to her patience, Adeline turned to face her mother. "I would never expect Dad to be so forgiving, or considerate of my feelings. Having Dad's blessing is something I've given up on long ago. So there's no need for you to warn me, Mom. I already know what's ahead of me."

The resolute tone to her voice must have caught Naomi's attention, because she walked over to Adeline and cupped a hand against the side of her face. "Adeline, this isn't like you. Quitting your job. Announcing a romance that I seriously doubt will last. And now this display of bitterness. I'm worried you're having some sort of emotional crisis."

Her "crisis" had been going on far longer than her mother could imagine. For years now her parents had ignored her pleas for independence. While she'd desperately needed their encouragement, instead, she'd gotten reasons why she wasn't capable of living without their guidance.

Two nights ago, when Maddox had offered her a marriage of convenience, he'd planted a seed of escape in her mind. And then when she'd overheard her coworkers repeating cruel falsehoods about her, it was like a cage door had been lifted, and she'd run through the opening as fast as she could. Now she was determined to keep moving forward. With or without her parents' approval.

"No crisis, Mom. I've just finally decided it's time for me to be me." She turned back to her closet and pulled out a dark blue sweaterdress with long fitted sleeves and a low, square neckline. As she carefully laid it over the back of a wing chair, she asked, "Is Dad home now?"

"No. He's out with the men and won't be back until lunchtime."

"Good. I'll have a talk with him then."

Naomi's groan was a sound of despair. "Is it really necessary to spring this on him now, Adeline? Can't it wait?"

"Wait for what?" She glanced over her shoulder to see her mother with a hand pressed against her forehead. "You know, last night I told Maddox I should break this to Dad gently. But now that I've talked with you and I've thought about it, that's really a stupid idea. Waiting isn't going to change things or make the situation any better. Today or two years from now, Dad is going to be his usual self."

Her mother huffed out a breath and started toward the door. "All right, Adeline. I'll leave you to have lunch with your father. I'm going to town to do some necessary shopping."

Adeline watched her mother close the door behind her before she slumped wearily onto the padded dressing bench.

Of course Naomi would find an excuse to leave the house. She'd never liked sitting in on family discussions. Mainly because Louis had never really allowed his wife to have a say in such matters. And when she did offer her opinion, it had to be in total agreement with her husband's. Otherwise, Louis would give his wife several days of the icy silent treatment.

Oh Lord, she should never feel guilty about entering into a marriage of convenience, Adeline thought. Not when her parents' relationship was a long way from normal.

Maddox was whistling under his breath while pushing the silver tiger-eye slide of a bolo tie up toward the collar of his hunter green shirt when Jameson knocked and stepped into the bedroom.

"Hey, big brother," Maddox greeted. "You made it back from the cattle auction?"

"Just now. I came by the house to give Dad a report, but Mom said he'd gone to see about the windmill in the west pasture. One of the hands said it stopped and he couldn't get it going."

"Oh. I didn't know anything about it," Maddox told him. "I was just about to head down to the kitchen to let Mom know I won't be home for dinner."

Jameson gave his brother a dry look. "I didn't

think you were getting all dressed up just to have dinner with the folks. Going out with your *special girl*?"

"Sure am. And her name is Adeline. Just in case you forgot."

"I didn't forget. Especially the Longsworth part. She's from a moneyed family, Maddox, but I'm sure that was the first thing you learned about her before you started dating. And by the way, just when did you two begin dating?"

Not about to let Jameson's little digs phase him, Maddox smiled. "Back in the summer. I first spotted her at the Fourth of July celebration in Bronco. At the pet contest, to be exact. Then, later, I literally bumped into her at the rodeo."

"On purpose, I'm sure."

Maddox chuckled. "Of course. A man has to think fast when he sees something he wants. Anyway, I talked her into giving me her phone number, and after that—well, we hit it off almost instantly."

Jameson folded his arms against his chest. "How easy—and convenient—for you."

Frowning, Maddox stepped away from the dresser mirror and reached for the wide leather belt lying on the end of the king-size bed.

"What's that supposed to mean?"

"Oh, nothing. Only that you've always been lucky where women are concerned."

"I'll tell you one thing, brother, this time I am truly lucky. Adeline is everything I've been looking for." Which was true enough, Maddox thought. If he wanted to get married for real, Adeline would be his first choice.

"So you really are serious about her? Or is this just one more of your short affairs? If it is, Maddox, I wish you wouldn't involve Mom and Dad. With you having Adeline here at the ranch to meet them, they're going to get the idea that she's an important fixture in your life."

"They'd be right," Maddox didn't hesitate to reply. "This isn't one of my short-term affairs, Jameson. Those days are over with for me. I'm in for the long haul with Adeline."

Jameson rolled his eyes and shook his head. "Not more than two weeks ago I overheard you talking with Dawson about a redhead you met at Doug's bar."

Chuckling, Maddox grabbed at the first thought that came through his mind. "Oh, her. Well, that was for his benefit. I thought he might get up his nerve and ask her for a date."

"Hmm. Well, this thing with Adeline, if it's real, then I wish you all the best, Maddox. If not, I hope she takes you for a hard ride."

A divorce after twelve months is not going to look good for either of us, or our families.

Adeline's comment suddenly came back to him, and he had to admit she was right. Jameson would no doubt take sheer joy in pointing out Maddox's failure as a husband. But by then none of Jameson's jabbing remarks would matter. Maddox would be the one holding the majority of the Double J.

"Thanks, brother. I wish you and Vanessa the best, too." He began to thread the belt through the loops of his jeans. "Only there's one difference between our well-wishes. I really mean it."

Frowning, Jameson walked over to him. "And you think I don't mean it? You got me wrong, Maddox. I do care. That's why I'm hoping like hell that you have changed your ways. Because I'd really hate to see you hurt that girl."

Hot anger spurted through him, even though he knew he had no right or reason to have such a reaction.

"Jameson, I don't try to tell you how to run your love life with Vanessa," he snapped. "So I'd appreciate if you'd let me worry about making Adeline happy."

"Sure, Maddox. I'll butt out. But if you ever need me—"

"I won't."

"Okay. See you tomorrow," Jameson said, then let himself out of the bedroom.

Once his brother was out of sight, Maddox walked over to the window and gazed out at the purple haze of twilight settling over the distant mountains and the cattle grazing in the nearby valley. The view had always filled Maddox with pride and joy, but now as he looked at the beauty of the land, he wondered if the ranch would ultimately be worth losing the trust of his brother, his family and friends.

If the truth of his and Adeline's marriage ever came out, they would all hate him. Could he live with that? Maybe not. But he sure as hell couldn't live with letting Jameson take everything, either.

But that was all wrong, Maddox thought ruefully. Jameson wasn't trying to take anything away from him. His brother hadn't asked to be named the major heir of the Double J. Randall had done that on his own. And no matter what eventually transpired with the inheritance, the last thing Maddox wanted was to have a wedge driven between him and his brother. He loved Jameson too much to let that happen.

During the drive into Bronco, Maddox tried to rid himself of the dark thoughts Jameson had raised in his mind, and thankfully by the time he met Adeline in the parking lot of DJ's Deluxe, he was back to his happy-go-lucky self.

"Wow! You look gorgeous!" he exclaimed as he helped her from her car. "You should've warned me you were going to dress up. I would've put on a sports jacket."

She smiled as she eyed the burgundy leather jacket he'd slipped on over his jeans and shirt. "Why? You look good in leather. I like it."

"Thanks. I've had this jacket for years. Guess you can tell by all the scars and worn spots. When I find something I like, I don't let go of it."

She pressed the key fob to lock her car, then dropped the device into a small clutch purse before she slanted him a pointed look.

"Hmm. You've surprised me. I took you for a man who prefers a frequent change."

Chuckling under his breath, he offered her his arm. "Only with some things."

Autumn had turned the nights even colder than usual in their part of Montana, and this evening Adeline had come prepared for the chill. She was wearing a faux fur jacket that resembled the coat of a snow tiger. The white fur made a lovely contrast to her dark hair, and as she slipped her arm through his, he was amazed at how easy it was to pretend he was in love with this woman.

Inside DJ's Deluxe, Maddox informed the hostess they were going to the bar for a cocktail before dinner.

"I want to show you off to Rusty," he said to Adeline as they made their way to the bar.

"Rusty? Is he a friend of yours?"

"I'd say so. He's the bartender. The one that was working the night you and I met. I told him then that I was going to marry you."

She stopped in her tracks and stared at him with a mixture of annoyance and disbelief. "Awfully sure of yourself, aren't you? If I remember correctly, that night I told you I wasn't interested in your proposal."

"Yes. But you let your friend believe we were— uh, a bit more than friends. That gave me hope."

"Hope? Sounds like it gave you a cocky dose of confidence."

Chuckling, he urged her forward. "A guy has to believe in himself to get ahead in the world."

When the two of them sat down at the bar, Rusty immediately walked over to them.

"Hello, Maddox. Nice to see you out this evening and with such a lovely lady." He gave a nod to Adeline. "Pleasure to see you again."

"Thank you. I'm Adeline Longsworth," she said, then added impishly, "Just in case Maddox didn't tell you my name while he was telling you he was going to marry me."

While Rusty laughed, Maddox lifted the back of her hand to his lips. "Adeline won't be a Longsworth for much longer. Right, darling?"

Her lips took on a provocative slant as she met his gaze. "You're going to have to hold your horses, sweetheart. It takes time to plan a huge wedding. And that is what you promised me, right?"

She was so perfect it was downright scary, Maddox thought as he kissed the soft skin of her hand for a second time. "Whatever your heart desires," he told her, then looked at Rusty and winked. "Love at first sight. It can really sweep a man off his feet. Better be careful, Rusty, or you might find yourself walking down the aisle."

The redheaded bartender awkwardly cleared his throat. "I'll leave that to you, Maddox," he said, then asked, "So what would you two like to drink to-night?"

They gave the man their orders, and after he'd left to mix the drinks, Adeline leaned slightly toward Maddox and said in a low voice, "You were spreading things on a bit thick, don't you think?"

He grunted with amusement. "The layer you were spreading on wasn't exactly thin," he said. "But I liked it."

She flashed him a clever grin. "After we end this charade, maybe I should go into acting. By then I'll have tons of experience."

He continued to hold her hand. For appearances' sake, of course. "We'll both be experts in the field."

The grin disappeared from her face. "I broke the news to my parents today—not that we're planning to get married soon, but that we're in love and serious."

"And what was their reaction?"

"To put it mildly, Mom is still in shock, and Dad is threatening to run you out of the state."

Maddox grunted. "The man must have delusions of grandeur."

Adeline sighed. "Dad has plenty of money, and he's closely acquainted with some powerful people. Therefore, he believes he can run roughshod over anyone he dislikes."

"Not me."

Her brown eyes regarded him for a long moment, and then she said, "No. I don't think you'd run scared like Spence."

Maddox had never met the man. There was no reason he should hate the sound of the guy's name. But each time Adeline spoke it, he wanted to curse.

"Spence was a fool," he muttered.

She looked at him in surprise. "You don't know him. How can you call him a fool?"

"I know what he gave up—you."

Her eyes searched his, and then suddenly her lashes fell, and as she turned her face away from him, he could see her throat move with a hard swallow.

Oh hell, surely she wasn't about to cry. She wasn't the type for tears, Maddox thought. But then maybe there were things about Adeline that he hadn't yet learned.

Placing a hand on her forearm, he asked, "Adeline, is something wrong?"

Turning back to him, she gave him a wry smile. "No. I'm just trying to figure out where your acting stops and reality begins. I doubt I'll ever know."

Did that really matter to her? He could understand why it might be important. Otherwise, she wouldn't be able to trust anything he said. Unless his words were put down in writing and certified with a notary stamp.

He said, "Listen, about Spence—I meant it. He was a fool not to fight for you."

She swiveled on the stool so that she was facing him. "Would *you* fight for me?"

"I have been, haven't I?"

The corners of her cherry-red lips curved downward. "Well, yes. But only for your personal gain. I wonder—"

"What?"

Just as he asked the question, Rusty arrived with their cocktails. Once the bartender had served them and moved on down the bar to check on another customer, Adeline shook her head.

"Nothing. It wasn't important." She reached for the stemmed glass in front of her. "Let's enjoy our drinks and talk about something pleasant. Like the coming Harvest Festival. Bronco always has fun things going on during the celebration. I can't wait to go. My friend Trudy mentioned there's even going to be a dance in the park this year."

Since many of Maddox's friends and acquaintances would be attending the Bronco Harvest Festival, it would be the perfect opportunity to show everyone he had a new woman on his arm—one who was making him forget all about his roaming bachelor ways.

"I can't think of anything I'd rather do than take you to all the fall festivities," he said with a grin.

Her laugh was mocking. "Sure. You look like the type of guy who'd enjoy bobbing for apples or drinking hot apple cider."

He feigned an offended look. "What are you talking about? I'm all hayseed. You're the one who doesn't fit at a pumpkin rolling. You're sitting there in a designer dress and fur."

Glancing down at her jacket, she exclaimed, "This is fake! And I'm not exactly in the middle of a pumpkin patch at the moment!"

"No matter. You look like you've just walked off a runway."

She frowned at him. "What's wrong with that? A few minutes ago you said I looked gorgeous."

"You are absolutely gorgeous tonight," he admitted. "But you don't exactly look like a rancher's wife."

Her jaw dropped at the same time her eyes widened. "Really?" she asked sarcastically. "My mother is a rancher's wife, and she dresses in designer clothing. Dad would hardly want her going around in burlap. What does your mother wear?"

The sarcasm in her voice drew a chuckle from him. "You know, your cheeks turn a real pretty pink when you get agitated."

"I wouldn't know. I don't go around looking at myself when I'm annoyed." She turned her stool away from him and took a long sip of her martini.

His chuckle turned to an indulgent smile. "Okay, Adeline. I'm sorry. I was only having some fun teasing you. It doesn't matter to me whether you wear fancy dresses or grubby jeans. As for what Mom wears, you saw her last night. She can dress up or down. Whatever the situation requires."

The frown on her face turned into an indulgent smile. "Honestly, Maddox, I was so on edge trying not to make a mistake about us, I can't remember what Mimi was wearing. A skirt and blouse of some sort, I think. I do recall that she looked nice."

"Thanks for complimenting her. And thanks for—" His words broke off as her gaze met his. Where was that soft, tender look in her eyes coming from? Moreover, why was he liking it?

"What? Agreeing to become your wife of convenience?" she asked with a mischievous grin.

No. Not a wife of convenience, but simply his wife, he thought. Thank God he'd stopped himself before he'd made that sort of mistake. She might have taken the slip of the tongue the wrong way, and the last thing he needed in this deal was for her to start thinking he was getting sentimental ideas about their marriage.

There wasn't going to be anything sentimental or romantic about their union, he reminded himself. There would be no tender feelings or sappy words of love. The vows they spoke at the altar would be as fake as Adeline's fur jacket.

Relieved that he'd set his thoughts back on the right track, he reached for her hand and squeezed it. "'Becoming my wife of convenience' was exactly what I was going to say. And you know something else? I'll be glad when I can slip a huge engagement ring on your finger. That way no one will make a mistake about our relationship."

She leaned her head close to his and lowered her voice. "And when do you plan on slipping this huge ring on my finger?"

She smelled like wildflowers on a hot June night, and suddenly he was wondering what it would be like to remove the jacket and slinky blue dress she was wearing and slide his hands over her slender curves, to hold her softness next to him.

The erotic thoughts were so vivid he was forced to clear his throat and glance away before he could manage to speak. "As soon as I can get to a jeweler," he told her. "Would you like to choose your ring, or do you want me to surprise you?"

She shrugged. "If our marriage was going to be the real thing and I'd be wearing the ring for years and years, I'd want us to choose it together. But since this thing with us is only temporary, anything will work."

For some reason, the word *temporary* bothered him, but so did the "years and years" comment. Adeline was a beautiful woman, but he couldn't envision himself waking up every morning and seeing her face on the pillow next to his. Or could he?

What the hell are you thinking, Maddox? Adeline will never be in your bed. Not as your fake wife or anything else. Burn that into the memory cells of your brain and everything will work out great.

Annoyed with the warning voice in his head, he tossed back the last of his whiskey and soda and hoped the alcohol would wash away his conscience or whatever it was that was making him think too much.

"Fine," he told her. "I'll choose a ring that befits a rich rancher's daughter."

"What about a rich rancher's wife?" she asked.

"Like you said, you'll only be my wife temporarily, but you'll always be Louis Longsworth's daughter." He placed his empty glass on the bar. "If you're finished with your drink, I think it's about time we had dinner."

She nodded. "Yes. I'm getting hungry."

So was he, Maddox thought. Hungry for all the wrong things.

Chapter Six

"Adeline, something weird is going on with you. First you tell me you've quit your job, and now this sudden urge for Western clothing! I've never seen you step foot in this store before. I think I should take your temperature. You're clearly not yourself."

Adeline glanced over at her friend Trudy. The tall redhead, who worked as a nurse in a local hospital, was staring at her with amazement. Which was hardly a surprise. Adeline didn't frequent any of Bronco's Western wear shops, but since she'd walked into this particular store, she'd already gathered up an armload of jeans, casual and fancy tops, and a tooled leather belt.

"I thought it would be fun to have some new

clothes. With the Bronco Harvest Festival coming up, I'll need something to wear."

Trudy burst out laughing, which caused a pair of female shoppers going through a nearby rack of prairie dresses to turn and look at them.

"Sorry," Trudy said as she tried to stifle her chuckles. "To hear you say you need something to wear is like me saying I need a piece of apple pie. Not after stepping on the bathroom scale this morning. And I've seen your walk-in closet. The rod is about to break just from the weight of your dresses alone!"

"That's just it, Trudy. For the past few years, I've mostly bought things to wear to work or pieces for dressy nights on the town," she explained as she motioned for her friend to follow her over to a long wall lined with endless shelves of cowboy boots.

You don't dress like a rancher's wife.

Adeline had never been embarrassed by her family's wealth. Nor had she ever believed she used her wardrobe to impress those around her. But two nights ago, when Maddox mentioned the way she'd been dressed in DJ's Deluxe, she'd been somewhat taken aback. He'd insisted he'd been teasing, but something in the tone of his voice had made her believe otherwise. And when she added his comment to the hurtful remarks she'd overheard her coworkers make in the restroom at Peak Experience Sports, she couldn't help but wonder if people did look at her as some sort of show-off.

Trudy said, "Because that's your life. But I can't

see where you'd need to buy all these things just for a harvest festival." She pointed at the clothing draped over Adeline's arm. "And cowboy boots? Come on! I know they're currently a fashion statement. Even famous actresses are wearing them. But you? You're a ballerina-flats and strappy-high-heels kind of woman."

Adeline could've told her friend that in recent days she'd also become an actress, and a darn good one at that. She'd practically convinced herself that she was happy. And why shouldn't she be, she asked herself. Soon, she'd be running her own business. She'd move away from the watchful eye of her father. She could date any man she wanted without worrying that Louis would put the scare in him.

Any man she wanted. After being married to Maddox, what man would want to follow in his footsteps? And where could she find a man who'd measure up to him?

Pushing the annoying questions from her mind, she gave Trudy a cheery smile. "I want to look good—like I fit in. And with the weather getting colder, a pair of boots will keep my feet warm."

Trudy's frown of disbelief grew even deeper. "Okay. Maybe I should be asking what is so all-fired important about this festival. I don't remember you attending any of the events last year."

"Right. Emily and I were in Idaho visiting relatives then. But my life is changing, Trudy. And I might as well explain things to you now, because you're going to find out anyway. I—uh, have been seeing someone, and he's planning for us to take in Bronco's festivities. That's why I want to be dressed appropriately."

Trudy appeared stunned—and rightly so. Only three weeks ago, Adeline had been wailing about Spence's sudden departure.

"When did this happen?"

Deciding not to put an unnecessary strain on her acting skills, Adeline turned to the shelved boots and began to search for her size. Trudy followed closely on her heels.

"Well, one thing is certain, you can't be serious about this new guy," Trudy continued in a dazed tone. "You haven't had time to get over Spence yet!"

Adeline tried not to groan out loud as she picked up a dark brown boot with fancy brown overlays stitched on the toe. "Wrong. I was over Spence long before he ever left for greener pastures. I just never told you about Maddox."

Trudy frowned. "Maddox? Should I recognize the name?"

Adeline smiled cleverly. "You remember the other night when you and I had dinner at DJ's Deluxe? You found me sitting at the bar with a man. Well, that was Maddox."

Trudy dramatically staggered backward, then sank onto a wide bench provided for customers to use when trying on boots.

"Him?" Trudy squeaked in disbelief. "That sexy dude with the dirty blond hair and long, lanky body?"

It was just like Trudy to have noticed the man's physique, Adeline thought wryly. She'd always been a little man-crazy, even though she'd been treated shabbily by more than one of her boyfriends.

"Yes. The sexy cowboy," Adeline told her.

Trudy's blue eyes widened. "When did you meet him?"

"We met during the Fourth of July celebration here in Bronco. And—well, it was sort of instant attraction."

Shaking her head in disbelief, Trudy glanced around to see if anyone was within earshot. "I don't get this, Adeline. You seemed so upset over Spence leaving. If you were already seeing the cowboy, why fret over Spence?"

Yes, this was the tricky part, Adeline thought. She didn't want to seem like a two-timer, but to her defense, she and Spence had never been engaged. They'd never even reached the serious stage.

Adeline carried the boot over to where Trudy was sitting and eased down next to her on the bench. "Spence was more of a good friend than anything," she explained. "And I was very angry with my parents for bullying him out of my life. It wasn't their place to send him packing. But as for Maddox, we— uh, we kept our relationship a secret until just a few days ago. That night you saw us at the bar, we were talking it over, and we decided then it was time to tell our families."

"But why the secrecy, Adeline? He's obviously quite a catch, and so are you."

Frowning, Adeline stared at the boot she was holding. "Well, you see, our fathers are not exactly bosom buddies. In fact, they feuded bitterly over a land grant. We—that is, Maddox and I were afraid they would resent the two of us being together and another row would start up all over again."

"I don't know Maddox John's father," Trudy said, "but I have met yours, and he isn't exactly a teddy bear."

Adeline's insides turned cold. "To no surprise, he's furious and making all sorts of threats."

"I hope you're not letting your dad sway you. Maybe that's something I shouldn't be saying, but I've been your friend for a long time now. Even when we were in elementary school together, I watched you struggle to always please him and your mother. Yes, they've given you material things, but I think they've held those things over your head. They want you to feel beholden. They want you to feel guilty if you don't follow their rules. That's not good, Adeline. And if the sexy cowboy makes you happy, then I say go for it!"

Happy. Funny, but even though this whole thing with her and Maddox was pretend, it did make her happy to be with him. And in the end, wasn't that all that really mattered? She had to think so.

Adeline gave her friend's shoulders a one-armed squeeze. "I intend to, Trudy. In fact, I'm driving out to the Double J to see him this afternoon."

"Lucky you."

"Yes, lucky me." Adeline piled the clothing she was holding into Trudy's lap, then, smiling with genuine pleasure, she kicked off her heel and pulled on the brown cowboy boot. As she held her foot out in front of her, she asked, "What do you think? Too much flash or not enough?"

Trudy laughed. "Why are you asking me? I'm a nurse. I spend most of my waking hours in thick crepe soles and scrubs. I'm hardly a fashionista."

"Can I help you ladies with something? A particular size or color of boot?"

Adeline and Trudy looked up to see a young woman standing in front of them. She was decked out in perfect cowgirl-chick fashion and smiling at both of them, as though she understood the two women were out of their element.

"I'd be grateful for your help," Adeline told her. "I'm looking for something to wear to the Bronco Harvest Festival. I want it to be nice but not too showy."

"She means luxury—understated," Trudy said with a knowing grin.

"Sure. I know exactly what she's looking for."

After trying on several pairs of boots and settling on a pair of brown ostrich hide with heels that added two inches to her height, Adeline paid for her purchases, then invited Trudy for a cup of coffee at Bronco Java and Juice.

Two hours later, Adeline drove the ten miles out of town to the Double J Ranch. When she'd texted Maddox that she was coming out to return his jean jacket, he'd told her to be there around three and he'd be waiting at the big tree near the corral.

Now, as the sight of the big barn came into view, she told her heart there was no reason for it to beat with happy anticipation, but it wouldn't listen. She hadn't seen Maddox since their dinner at DJ's Deluxe, and foolish or not, she had to admit she'd missed him.

When she parked her car in an out-of-the-way spot near the corral fence, she glanced at the digital clock on the dashboard to see she was five minutes early.

Since Maddox was nowhere in sight, she grabbed a suede jacket from the back seat and left the car. As she walked toward the big cottonwood, she noticed more of the yellow leaves had fallen to create a carpet around the wooden bench beneath it.

She took a seat on the side where she could see the working area beyond the barn. A pair of cowboys were cleaning water troughs, while in an adjoining pen another was spreading blocks of alfalfa hay into a long manger.

"Hello, pretty lady."

At the sound of Maddox's voice, she turned to see him walking up behind her. He was dressed all in denim, and judging by the dust coating his clothes and black hat, he'd been working hard. However, it was the sight of his smiling face that her gaze was focused on, and before she realized what she was doing, she jumped to her feet and threw her arms around his neck.

"Wow! What's this about?" he asked with a surprised laugh.

"We have an audience," she whispered, then planted a kiss on one cheek and then the other.

"Well, now, that makes everything different," he whispered back. "Let's give the guys something to really talk about."

His arms wrapped around her and squeezed her so tightly against his chest, it nearly squished the air from her lungs. She was trying to regain her breath when his lips came down on hers, and then all of a sudden, filling her lungs with oxygen became a mere afterthought.

This kiss was equally earth-shattering to Adeline as the one he'd given her on the porch a few days ago. Only this one felt as if it would never end. And, shockingly, she didn't want it to.

When he finally lifted his head and eased her back from him, she gulped in a long breath and tried to sound cool and calm. "You must have really wanted to put on a show."

He grinned. "You were doing a whale of a job helping me, too."

Adeline blushed while wondering what he must be

thinking. That she was actually getting sweet feelings about him? No. He thought she was playacting, and she had to make herself believe that's all he was doing, too.

She laughed lightly in an effort to mask her shaken senses. "I was only elaborating on the fact that I've missed you. Strange, isn't it? A few days ago, I didn't even know you. But you make for good company."

Her comment appeared to surprise him. "I think you actually mean that."

"I do."

Placing a hand against her back, he urged her toward the bench. "Let's sit down," he suggested. "I have something to show you."

"I have something to show you, too," she said as they took a seat close together on the worn boards. "It's in the car. You can see them when I get your jacket."

"Them?" he laughed. "You have someone hidden in the back seat?"

"No. My friend and I went shopping today in Bronco, and I bought a few things for the Harvest Festival. You do still plan for us to go, right?"

"I wouldn't miss it. Especially now." The corners of his eyes crinkled with a smile as he reached inside his brown twill work jacket and pulled out a small velvet box. "I went shopping, too."

Her heart was suddenly hammering with excitement. Which was such a silly reaction. None of this was real. Except that Maddox's big, masculine presence seemed very real. And so had that whopper of a kiss a moment ago.

"Oh." She breathed the one word as she stared at the box. "You went ring shopping."

"Sure did. I visited Beaumont and Rossi's jewelry shop in Bronco Heights today. And I hope you're not disappointed." He pushed up the tiny lid and held the jewelry box out for her to view. "What do you think?"

Adeline's gasp was not only genuine, it was loud as she stared in wonder at the large emerald-cut diamond, flanked by four smaller stones and set on a white filigree band. Even in the irregular lighting beneath the shade of the tree, she could see the diamonds were flawless and had no doubt cost a small fortune.

"Maddox, it's beautiful! But I wasn't expecting anything this extravagant! I only hope that once this is over, you can get most of the money back."

He darted her an odd look before he took the ring from its velvet bed and reached for her hand. "It's a one-of-a-kind ring. The band is hand-carved platinum. I paid the jeweler extra for him to rush sizing it to fit your finger."

Her heart still pounding at a ridiculous rate, Adeline straightened out her fingers so that he could slip the ring into place.

"It's perfect, Maddox. I don't know what to say—except that I'm stunned. I mean, if you were really my fiancé, I'd be kissing you and telling you how much I love you. But as it is, about all I can say is thank you for wanting me to look properly engaged."

He grimaced as his gaze connected with hers. "Damn it, Adeline, you are properly engaged. I've proposed, you have the ring and we are getting married. That's all very real. Maybe you'll be more convinced if we give the ranch hands another show—just for good measure," he added slyly.

Adeline's lips parted as she darted a glance toward the corral where the cowboys were still working. "Uh, don't you think they've had enough *show* for one afternoon?"

Chuckling under his breath, he wrapped a thumb and forefinger over her chin and dragged her face back to his. "Not nearly enough, Adeline. In a few minutes, we're going to start spreading the news that we've just gotten engaged. Everyone will expect us to behave as though we're totally besotted with each other."

"Oh," she said in a breathless rush. "Then I suppose we'd better make this look good."

"That's my girl," he murmured.

Before Adeline could calm her racing heart or prepare herself for another one of his kisses, he was drawing her into a tight embrace. The instant his lips met hers, some sort of magical fog settled over her. Instinctively, her eyelids drifted downward, and there was nothing make-believe in the way her arms wrapped around his neck or the way her lips parted eagerly to the hungry search of his mouth.

By the time he finally eased his head back from

hers, Adeline was so lost in his kiss that all she could do was stare at him in stunned fascination.

"Do you feel properly engaged now?"

The husky sound of his voice drew her gaze to the wry slant of his lips, and in spite of the thrill his kiss had just given her, she realized he didn't have a serious bone in his body. Not when it came to their relationship, or their coming marriage. The only thing he was serious about was acquiring the major share of this enormous ranch.

And why should that fact make you feel melancholy, Adeline? You're no different. You're in this for the money. So just think about what you're going to do with it, and in the meantime enjoy the man's kisses and forget about the motive behind them.

Disgusted with the mocking advice echoing in her head, Adeline locked her gaze on the diamonds sparkling up at her. "I feel like we're actually headed toward the wedding your father has been wishing for."

He gently patted her cheek, and Adeline was horrified at the lump of emotion suddenly choking her.

"You bet we are," he said with happy enthusiasm. "Dad went into the house a few minutes ago for a coffee break. We'll probably find him and Mom in the den. Let's go give them the news."

Oh, Lord, she wasn't sure she was ready to go through another acting scene with Maddox. But somehow she had to get ready. Now that she was wearing his engagement ring, there was no way she could leave the ranch without first seeing his parents.

"Do you think they'll be surprised?" Adeline asked.

He helped her up from the bench, then wrapped an arm around her waist. "Probably. But the key is to make them believe we're truly serious. And given that they've heard me vow to be a bachelor for the rest of my life, it's going to be a tough sell on my part." He urged her toward the house. "But I'm counting on them taking a good look at you and understanding how I came to change my mind."

She let out a good-natured groan. "A cowboy con man, Maddox. That's what you are."

He slapped a hand over the region of his heart. "You've really wounded me, Adeline."

She cast him an overly sweet smile. "How does that old saying go—don't kid a kidder? Well, I'm fairly certain that whatever I say isn't going to penetrate the cold steel around your heart."

As soon as she made the comment, she expected him to come back with an angry retort. But she was pleased when he merely chuckled.

"There's a lot you still need to learn about your fiancé. Especially before you marry me."

After the way she'd practically melted beneath his kiss, she was beginning to think there were a bunch of things she needed to learn about herself.

Randall and Mimi weren't nearly as surprised by his engagement as Maddox had expected them to be. In fact, they appeared to be overjoyed with the news.

After a round of hugs and congratulations, Randall said, "I think this news calls for a toast. Since it's cold out today, Mimi, why don't you break out that bottle of brandy the Abernathys gave us for an anniversary gift?"

"Sounds perfect," Mimi told him.

She was walking over to a bar of polished pine when a male voice called out from an open doorway.

"Knock, knock. Are we invited to this little party?"

Maddox stifled a groan as he turned to see Jameson and his fiancée entering the room. What were they doing showing up at this time of the afternoon? Had they been passing through the ranch yard and been overcome with curiosity when they spotted Adeline's car?

"Jameson! Vanessa! You two couldn't have stopped at a better time!" Randall exclaimed. "Come join us. We were just about to have a toast."

The couple walked over to where Maddox, Adeline and Randall were standing in front of the fireplace, soaking up the warmth of the burning logs.

"What kind of toast?" Jameson's curious gaze scanned the group. "Are we buying more cattle?"

"There is more to life than cattle, big brother. I just gave Adeline an engagement ring, and she's accepted my proposal of marriage," Maddox told him while taking huge delight in the stunned expression on his brother's face.

"What?" Jameson practically shouted the question while Vanessa politely stepped forward and gave Maddox a huge hug.

"Congratulations, brother-in-law-to-be," she said to him, then smiled at Adeline. "And I'm fairly certain I haven't met my new sister-in-law-to-be. Would you introduce us?"

"My pleasure," Maddox told her, then proudly hugged Adeline to his side. "This is Adeline Longsworth. Perhaps you might know her parents, they own the Lazy L. And Adeline, this is Vanessa Cruise. She teaches science at Bronco High School and her brother owns Bronco Ghost Tours."

The two women exchanged greetings and shook hands.

"I've always planned to take one of those ghost tours," Adeline said, "but I just never had the time."

"You really should," Vanessa told her. "They're fun and informative, too."

"Don't you mean a bit inventive, sweetheart?" Jameson asked his fiancée in a teasing voice.

The lovely brunette laughed softly. "To some degree, the stories are imaginative," she admitted. "But each tour is based on a legend that's been passed on through the years."

"Adeline is a travel agent," Maddox spoke up. "She plans trips for CEOs and other businesspeople who are too lazy to do it themselves."

"Maddox! That's a hell of a way to describe your fiancée's work!" Randall scolded him. "She must like the work or she wouldn't be doing it."

Maddox saw Adeline's lips press tightly together before she turned a strained smile on his father. "Actually, I'm in between jobs right now, Randall. That is, I plan to start up my own agency soon. Right now, though, I'm more interested in focusing on my relationship with Maddox."

"Sounds like a lovely idea to me, Adeline." Mimi said as she approached the group carrying a tray filled with six snifters and a decanter of brandy. "You can always work at a job later on."

Jameson chuckled slyly. "You mean after she's married and the children arrive? If they take after Maddox, then Adeline will need all the me time she can get."

Him, a father? To Adeline's children? Maddox's imagination couldn't jump that far into the future. And even if it could, he wouldn't see Adeline or a passel of little ones gathered around his feet.

A few steps away, Mimi placed the tray on a nearby side table and proceeded to pour the brandy. She said, "Vanessa better hope your children don't take after you, Jameson. The way I remember things, you were just as rowdy as Maddox."

Vanessa laughed and so did Adeline, yet even though Maddox realized his mother was teasing, he couldn't summon a sound of amusement. He was too busy thinking about how things would be after his divorce. How soon would it be before Adeline married for real and started having some other man's babies? And why did that idea sicken him?

Listen, you fool, just because you'll have a marriage license saying Adeline is your wife, that doesn't mean you'll have any claims on her. Especially her heart.

"Maddox! Wake up! This toast is for you and Adeline, remember?"

Jameson's voice finally penetrated the confusion going on in Maddox's head, and he felt a rush of embarrassed heat crawl up his face as he recognized his mother was standing in front of him, waiting for him to take his glass from the tray.

"Oh. Sorry, Mom. I was thinking."

"Who would've guessed," Jameson remarked in a droll voice.

Maddox shot him an annoyed look before he turned his gaze on his father. "Actually, I was thinking about you, Dad. When you and Mom first got engaged and whether you felt anything like I'm feeling right now."

Smiling smugly, Randall reached out and curled an affectionate arm around his wife's shoulders. "I don't know how you're feeling, son, but I felt like I could jump over the moon while dragging a cow behind me."

"Oh, Randall, why are you lying to your sons and future daughters-in-law?" Mimi lovingly scolded her husband. "When I said yes to your proposal, you were so shaken up that you ran out of the house and halfway to the barn before you realized you'd forgotten to kiss me."

"Well, I made up for it, didn't I?" Randall said to his wife, then added, "And, Maddox, you have a good reason to daydream. You're in love. Jameson can tell you now that he has Vanessa in his life, he has his own problems staying focused."

Jameson chuckled as he slanted a loving look at his fiancée. "Okay, I'll confess. It's hard to think about anything except her."

His brother's comment put a glowing smile on Vanessa's face. At the same time, Maddox could feel Adeline studying his own expression. What was she thinking? Was she wishing their relationship was the real deal? No. Her dad was a rancher, but Maddox couldn't picture Adeline falling for a cowboy. She was the sort who'd eventually wind up married to a successful businessman with plenty of money and a mini-mansion in the suburbs.

"Well, now that we all have our glasses," Randall said, lifting his snifter, "let's drink to Maddox and Adeline. May their love be eternal, and may it bring them much happiness and many children."

Beaming a smile at Maddox and Adeline, Mimi said, "I will certainly drink to that."

Vanessa seconded the woman's wishes. "Yes, I wish you both much love and happiness."

Jameson swiftly added, "Same here, little brother. And to you, too, Adeline."

After everyone had taken a sip of the brandy, Maddox turned to Adeline and was instantly knocked for a loop. Her brown eyes were glazed with tears, and his first thought wasn't to question whether they were genuine or not—it was to console her.

"Adeline? Sweetheart, are you crying?" Hugging her closer to his side, he pressed a kiss to her temple. "This is supposed to be a joyous occasion."

She sniffed and gave him a wobbly smile. "It's not every day a girl gets engaged. I'm a bit overwhelmed with emotion."

Before Maddox could reassure her, Mimi rushed over and gave her a hug.

"Of course it's natural to shed a few happy tears on a day like this. And we're all thrilled about this, Adeline," Mimi told her. "Maddox has finally found his soul mate and wants to settle down. You should be happy—you've worked a miracle."

Everyone laughed at Mimi's remark, except for Maddox. He was too busy wondering if the snowball he and Adeline had started rolling was going to grow into something too large for either of them to handle.

It's too late to start worrying now, Maddox. Instead, take a long look at your brother and remember if you don't pull off this charade, he'll end up with the major share of the Double J.

The voice running through Maddox's head had him glancing over to Jameson. With only two years' difference in their ages, they'd been inseparable as boys. Maddox had always looked up to his big brother, and even now with the inheritance issue standing between them, Maddox's deep love for Jameson hadn't changed. Still, he couldn't stand by and let his brother take over the reins of the ranch. It wasn't right or fair.

But is it right or fair for you to have the majority, Maddox?

If the tiny voice between his ears was his conscience, then he was going to kick it aside, Maddox thought. He couldn't afford to allow ethics or morality to guide him now.

The afternoon was growing late by the time Adeline finally convinced Maddox she needed to head home to the Lazy L. After telling his parents goodbye, he walked her out to where she'd parked her car near the cottonwood tree.

As they stood beside the driver's door, he said, "I really wish you would have agreed to stay for dinner, Adeline. Considering that we just announced our engagement, it would've made everything look more convincing."

His remark caused her raw nerves to suddenly snap, and she looked at him with angry amazement. "Convincing? Don't you think I've done enough for one day? I'm exhausted from this—this farce! I'm sorry, but I can't do any more of it tonight!"

For a long, silent stretch, he stared at her, and then his eyes narrowed to skeptical slits. "Are you going soft on me, Adeline?"

Her heart was suddenly pounding, and she wished she'd held her temper in check. Because she didn't want Maddox to dig into her true feelings. Not now or ever.

"What do you mean?"

A smirk tugged at his lips. "I mean this subterfuge is becoming too much for you to handle emotionally. Earlier this afternoon, after my family toasted our engagement, those were real tears in your eyes, Adeline. Don't try to deny it."

She gasped with outrage. "Why would I try to deny it? Of course they were real tears! And why not? Was there something wrong with me displaying a little true emotion?" she asked hotly. "Sorry, Maddox, but I'm not a robot! Your family has been kind and nice to me. It felt good to have them accept me—approve of me—even if none of this is real to you. But I doubt you'd understand anything about a person's feelings. All you understand is getting your hands on sections of grazing land and thousands of head of cattle!"

Her outburst must have taken him by surprise, because he stared at her in amazement for what seemed like an eternity before he finally glanced away and drew in a deep breath.

"You're right. I apologize, Adeline. No doubt this has been hard on you, and I shouldn't be asking so much of you so quickly," he said quietly.

She sighed as a feeling of remorse washed over her. It wasn't her nature to lash out at anyone. If it had been, she would've stepped out of the bathroom stall that day she'd overheard her ex-coworkers gossiping about her and blasted them with angry truths. "I'm sorry, too, Maddox. The ring, announcing our engagement—it's put us under a lot of pressure. And I still have to go through all this with my parents. And believe me, they're not going to take the news like Randall and Mimi did."

He turned his gaze back to her, and the soft look in his blue eyes sent a pang of longing and regret right through the middle of her chest.

"Is there anything I can do to help you deal with them? If you're not ready to tell them about our engagement, then do it later," he told her. "You can always slip off the ring whenever you're around them."

Adeline shook her head. "No. Even before you gave me the ring today, I had already made up my mind. I'm not going to hold anything back from them. It's time they accept the choices I make with my life. If they can't respect my decisions, then I can survive without their blessings."

He shook his head. "I wish things were different for you. And I don't mean this thing with you and me. I'm talking about your parents. I've never met them, but I can see they've caused you some unhappiness. I don't like the idea that I'm giving them reason to cause you more of the same."

Oh dear, maybe it would have been easier on her if he'd remained indifferent to her feelings. Now all she wanted to do was throw her arms around him and thank him for being so understanding.

Swiping her long, tangled hair away from her

face, she let out a weary breath. "Don't worry about it. If they didn't have you or our engagement to harp about, they'd find something else. You know, I envy my sister being away in Billings."

His gaze made a sweeping study of her face. "Is that what you'd like to do once this marriage of ours has ended? Move away from the Bronco area?"

She shrugged while realizing she didn't like thinking that far ahead. She didn't like imagining how her life would be without Maddox in it.

Oh God, she needed help, she thought. She'd only known this man for a few short days, and yet she already felt herself being drawn deeply into his life—and to him.

"I'm not sure. That's too far ahead to know how I'll be thinking or feeling."

"You're right. Thinking too far ahead can get a person in trouble." He gave her a brief smile, then attempted to peer through the darkened window of her car. "When you first arrived this afternoon, you said you had something to show me. Still want to show me?"

Had it only been this morning when she and Trudy had been shopping in the Western store? So much had happened she felt like days had passed rather than hours.

"Oh. I almost forgot. Since you said I don't dress like a rancher's daughter—or wife—I bought these." She opened the car door and pulled the boot box from the back seat. "They felt really comfy when I tried them on. It's no wonder you cowboys always stick to wearing boots."

"I'd feel silly in anything else," he admitted. "But you, in boots? I'm surprised. Or, let me guess, you picked out fashion boots that sort of have a Western flair?"

With a clever smile, she placed the box on the hood of the car and pulled out one of the boots for him to see. "No way. Unlike our engagement, these are the real deal. What do you think?"

"Woo-hoo!" he exclaimed with a wide grin. "Now that is a pair of snazzy boots."

His reaction made her happy, and before she could think about it, she slipped her arms around his waist and hugged him. "Thanks, Maddox. Now when people see us together at the Bronco Harvest Festival, we'll look like a ranching couple instead of an odd couple."

He picked up her hand and tilted it until the nearby yard lamp caught the glitter of her diamond ring. "Not only that, we'll look like an engaged couple. Is that going to make you feel guilty?"

Her smile was wan. "No. It's going to make me feel proud. What about you?"

"Very proud," he murmured, then before she could guess his intentions, he lowered his head and placed a soft kiss on her lips.

"What was that for?" she asked once the contact had ended and she glanced beyond his shoulder toward the barn area. "I don't see any of the ranch hands around at the moment."

"The kiss wasn't for the ranch hands," he told her. "It was a thank-you. For not staying angry with me. And for having the courage to become my wife."

This was the moment when she needed to laugh and make light of his words, but try as she might, she couldn't express any sort of humor.

"You think being your wife requires courage?" she asked.

"Sure. I'm arrogant and stubborn and expect to get my way all the time. Oh, I should add selfish, too. I'm usually thinking of myself instead of others."

She managed to give him a lopsided grin. "In other words, you're a typical man," she teased.

His eyes met hers, and Adeline's heart reacted with a hard thump.

"Yeah. But I don't think you're going to have any problem handling me."

"No problems at all," she agreed. "Because I have no intentions of ever *handling* you."

Certain he was going to come back with a sharp retort, she was more than surprised when a faint smile tugged at the corners of his lips. "Good night, Adeline. I'll call you tomorrow and we'll make plans—so you can wear those boots."

He turned, and as he walked back to the house, Adeline hurriedly tossed the boot box into the car, then climbed into the driver's seat.

Thankfully, he hadn't realized she'd been putting

on an act with him, she thought as she put the car in gear and gunned it the direction of town. He'd had no idea how the urge to kiss him again had been surging through her, or how much she'd wanted to press her cheek against his chest and let the warmth of his body spread through hers.

Yes, she'd fooled him with her cool act. But she was also fooling herself if she thought for one minute that she could become Maddox's wife and not end up making love to him.

Chapter Seven

"Adeline, I'm very disappointed in you. For twenty-five years, I've tried to guide you in the right direction. To keep you on a path that would lead you to wealth and success. But instead of sticking to your father's advice, you take off on some sentimental venture that's only going to bring you misery. I hope you realize just how opposed I am to this—this…" Louis Longsworth slashed a hand through the air as he stared down the long dining table to where his daughter was attempting to eat breakfast. "This ridiculous engagement!"

Adeline gripped the handle of the fork tightly as she pushed it into a mound of scrambled eggs on her plate. The eggs were cooked hard. Just the way her father liked them. Everything Naomi cooked, every decision and move she'd ever made, she'd done to please him and him only.

Perhaps Adeline was too forward-thinking. Maybe her mother's way was how a wife had to be in order to hold a marriage together for years and years. But weren't there times a wife should be a mother first and stick up for her children's happiness?

Last night, after she'd returned from the Double J, Adeline had gone straight to her parents and showed off the impressive ring Maddox had slipped onto her finger. As expected, Louis had exploded with threats of disowning her and ruining Maddox's life. Now he'd started off this morning with the same lecture.

Drawing in a weary breath, Adeline said, "Yes, Dad. I understand you're disappointed with me. But that's nothing new."

Louis tossed down his fork, making the utensil clatter against the oak tabletop. "And another thing," he barked. "If you think I'm going to put up with your sarcasm, you're sadly mistaken. You obviously have your own ideas about what is right or wrong, but I rule this house, Adeline."

From the corner of her eye, she could see her mother's lips were pressed into a tight line, but Adeline knew she wouldn't say a word.

"You're right, Dad. This is *your* home." Rising to her feet, Adeline picked up her plate, which still held the majority of her meal. "Thanks for the breakfast, Mom. It was delicious."

With her father glaring at her, Adeline left the dining room. In the kitchen, she scraped and washed her plate, then went straight upstairs to her bedroom and stepped into the shower.

Earlier, she'd found a text on her phone from Trudy informing her that her shift at the hospital had changed. She'd be working all day and wouldn't be able to meet Adeline for lunch.

The news had already added to her heavy spirits. Now, more than ever, she needed someone to talk to. Trouble was, she couldn't tell Trudy what was really going on in her life. Yes, she could show off her engagement ring and give her the news that she and Maddox would be getting married sooner rather than later. But the phoniness of the engagement and the genuine feelings she was beginning to have toward the sexy cowboy were things she'd have to keep to herself.

Thirty minutes later, she was switching off the blow dryer when she heard her cell phone ring.

Thinking it might be Maddox, she hurried out of the bathroom and across the bedroom to where she'd left the phone on the window seat.

The caller turned out not to be Maddox but her sister, Emily. She managed to swipe the accept button before Emily hung up.

"Hey, little sissy, what's up?" she answered in the most cheerful voice she could muster.

Emily's reply was a clever chuckle. "Unlike you, I have nothing but books and tests in my life. So why haven't I gotten a call from you already? Why was Mom the first to tell me about your engagement?"

Easing onto the padded window seat, Adeline looked outside at the clouds gathering over the mountaintops and the wind whipping the fallen leaves across the backyard. The kidney-shaped swimming pool had been covered more than six weeks ago, and the lawn furniture from the adjoining patio was now stacked away in storage. Winter weather and Christmas weren't that far away, she thought. Would she and Maddox be married by then?

The inner question brought her gaze to the lavish diamonds on her finger. Obviously he could afford the dazzling piece of jewelry, but she hadn't expected him to buy her anything so extravagant. Any decent diamond would've worked. Why had he gone so overboard? To impress his friends? Or to please her?

Adeline groaned as she attempted to push away the questions running through her mind and answer her sister. "I should've known Mom would call you before I had a chance to tell you myself."

"Well, she did. So now I want to hear all the good parts from you."

Adeline drew her legs up under her and leaned a shoulder against the back of the seat. "Good parts? What do you mean?"

"Oh, come on, sis! What does this guy look like? Where did you meet? And why in the world haven't I heard about him before now?" She paused to draw in a breath but went on before Adeline had a chance to answer even one question. "The last I heard you were moping over Spence leaving town. Now all of a sudden you're engaged! Is this really my sensible sister?"

Adeline momentarily closed her eyes as feelings of guilt rushed over her. She hated the fact that she had to mislead Emily. But one day, after Emily learned the real reason she agreed to marry Maddox, she knew her sister would ultimately understand her decision.

"I'll have to snap a pic of Maddox and send it to you. Or maybe you remember seeing him around Bronco. He's one of the John brothers. Jameson, Maddox and Dawson. And they have a younger sister, Charity. She's around your age, in fact. I haven't met her or Dawson yet, but I'm sure I will soon."

Emily went quiet for a moment, and from the voices in the background, Adeline decided she was somewhere on campus.

"The Johns," Emily said thoughtfully. "The name sounds very familiar. Oh! I got it—they were at a charity event I attended. It had something to do with orphans and Christmas gifts, I think. I don't remember seeing a sister, but I do recall the three brothers. They were all hunky cowboys."

Adeline smiled at her sister's description. "Yes, Maddox is quite a hunk. Dreamy blue eyes and dirty blond hair and dimples to go with a pair of luscious lips. Does that sound acceptable to you?"

Emily sighed, then giggled. "Leave it to you, Adeline. You always did attract the best ones. I can't wait to meet him!" she exclaimed. Then in a somber tone she added, "But from what Mom says, she doesn't expect Dad to let the guy in the house. Do you think that will change before I come home for Christmas break?"

"I wouldn't hold my breath," Adeline told her. "But don't worry—we'll all three get together."

There was a long pause, and then Emily sighed. "Are you wildly in love with him?" she asked, then giggled as though she'd asked the silliest of questions. "That was stupid of me. Of course you're wildly in love with him. You'd hardly marry anyone you didn't love."

"Yes. I'm—uh, pretty wild about Maddox. We haven't known each other all that long. But it was one of those instant things, Emily. When I saw him the first time, I was blown away. And I still am." Which was true enough, Adeline thought. Just looking at Maddox was enough to make her heart race and her breath catch in her throat.

"Hmm. I'll bet he was blown away with you, too. That's the way it is with you, Adeline. Men take one look at my big sister and they don't know I exist."

Adeline laughed. Emily's features and dark hair resembled Adeline's, only she was more petite and her personality far more vivacious. "Sure, sweetie. You've already had too many boyfriends to count. I'll bet you have a special one right now."

"As a matter of fact, I do. But don't tell Dad. I don't want him giving me the problems he's been giving you."

"Don't worry. I'm going to be avoiding Dad as much as possible," Adeline told her. "And your love life is your business, sissy. Not his."

"I plan to keep it that way, too. Sorry you're having problems with Dad, Adeline. But let's face it, as long as you're living on the Lazy L, he's going to try to call all the shots. Hopefully after you're married, your husband will set him straight on the matter. And, by the way, have you set a date for the wedding yet?"

The mere thought of donning a bridal gown and exchanging vows of love with Maddox was enough to tie her nerves into knots. "Not yet. Maddox only gave me a ring yesterday. It's too soon for all those plans."

"Not for me! I—" Emily's words were suddenly interrupted by a faint buzzing noise. "Oh, darn it! That's the alarm on my smart phone. I have to head to class, Addie. Take a close-up pic of your ring and send it to me. I'm betting it's really fab!"

"Oh, it's fab, all right," she said with a little laugh. "'Bye, Emily. I love you."

"Love you, too! Congratulations, sissy!"

The signal ended, and Adeline rose and crossed the room to where she'd laid out the clothes she was planning to wear to town.

Actually, now that Trudy couldn't make the lunch date, there wasn't any need for her to drive into town.

But the thought of staying here all day and chancing another run-in with her father was enough to flatten her spirits. She'd find something to do. Even if it meant spending the whole afternoon in the library.

She was stepping into a brown suede midi skirt when her mother knocked and stepped into the bedroom.

"Oh, you're going out?" Naomi asked as she watched Adeline slip a cropped camel-colored sweater over her head.

"I'm going in to Bronco to do lunch and a bit of shopping."

Naomi pointedly checked her watch as though Adeline needed to be reminded it was still early. "I see. Well, I only wanted to ask you something."

Adeline walked over to a cheval mirror and adjusted the hem of the sweater at her waistline. "About Maddox, I imagine," she replied tersely. "I had hopes I'd get congratulations from you and Dad. Instead I get drilled and berated. How do you think that makes me feel? Is that how you were treated when you got engaged to Dad?"

For once Naomi looked ashamed, and in that moment Adeline hated herself. She should be bigger than this. It was pointless to try to change or shame her parents for the way they were treating her. They would never change. She needed to focus entirely on the future and how Maddox was going to help her gain her freedom.

"No. Honestly, my parents were happy for me,"

Naomi admitted. "And we would be happy for you, too, Adeline, if only—"

Adeline swiftly held up her hand. "Please don't start, Mom. There is no man in the state of Montana, much less the United States, whom Dad would find acceptable to be my husband. Furthermore, you know I'm right. So let's not go into if-onlys."

Naomi lifted her chin to a defensive angle. "Okay. I came up here because I was wondering—you haven't mentioned any kind of engagement party. Are Maddox's parents going to give you one?"

An engagement party? The idea wasn't something she and Maddox had discussed while they'd been making their marriage plans. Although now that Naomi had mentioned it, Adeline suspected the Johns would certainly want to make a big show of announcing Maddox's engagement.

"I have no idea what their plans might be. Why?"

Naomi sighed, and Adeline didn't miss the wistful note in her mother's expression. All these years of living with Louis had taught her to hide her real feelings and thoughts. Many times Adeline had wondered what kind of personality her mother would truly have if she let everyone see the real Naomi.

She said, "I was thinking how nice it would be if your father would agree to have a party for you here on the Lazy L. You *are* our daughter."

Surprised by her mother's suggestion, Adeline walked over to where Naomi stood rigidly next to a wing chair.

"Mom, you are not thinking! Dad isn't going to give me anything. You heard him last night and this morning. I imagine he's already called the family lawyer to have me taken out of the will."

Naomi gasped. "Adeline! That's an awful thing to say!"

"Sometimes the truth is awful, Mom."

"Your father doesn't want to punish you financially."

Punish wasn't exactly the correct word, Adeline thought. It was more like he wanted to extort and bend her to his will.

"Mom, please don't bother trying to make everything seem better than it really is. Besides, what Dad does with his wealth is his business. I don't need or want his money. Yes, I once asked him for a loan, but he couldn't even see fit to give me that. And now—well, I figure he'd rather endure a root canal without Novocain than acknowledge that I'm going to become Maddox John's wife."

Naomi blinked then turned her attention to the opposite side of the room. "Oh, Adeline, there's no need for you to be so bitter. If—"

Not wanting to cause her mother any more distress, she gently placed a hand on her shoulder. "Mom, you're right. From today forward, I'm going to leave the bitterness behind. I'm going to be married and start a new life. I'm going to be happy. And if Maddox's parents do decide to give us some sort of engagement party, I'm sure they'd be glad for you to attend."

Naomi turned a hopeful expression on Adeline. "Do you think so?" she asked, then just as quickly her features drooped with doubts. "Louis was like a bulldog when he went after that land grant. I doubt the Johns have forgotten the way he treated them."

"They might not have forgotten, but they've forgiven."

A measure of relief crossed Naomi's face, but the expression was short-lived. "I could never attend without your father. It would cause a scandal. Along with making your father furious. I'm not even sure he'll give in and attend your wedding. I don't want to miss seeing you get married, Adeline. You're my daughter!"

As Adeline studied the dejected look on her mother's face, she suddenly understood that Naomi had never stood up for her daughters, or even herself, because she lacked the courage to do so. And the knowledge very nearly broke Adeline's heart.

"Oh, Mom." Wrapping an arm around her shoulders, she hugged her tightly. "We'll worry about all that when the time comes. As long as I know you love me, that's all that matters."

"Adeline," she said in a voice thick with emotion, "maybe there are times it doesn't seem like I care, but I do. I love you very much. Don't ever forget that."

Adeline pressed a kiss on her cheek. "I won't."

Naomi gently patted Adeline's arm. "Go on and enjoy your trip to town, dear."

"Thanks, Mom. I will."

Naomi watched her mother leave the bedroom, and then, without warning, she dropped her head in her hands and sobbed.

For the first time she could remember, her mother had given her a glimpse of her true self and opened her heart just enough for Adeline to see inside. The breakthrough should have been something for her to celebrate. Instead it made her sick to know her mother's revelation had come about because of a lie. Naomi wanted to be a part of a wedding that had nothing to do with love and everything to do with financial gain.

Dear God, she and Maddox were no better than her father, she thought sickly.

Are you going soft on me, Adeline?

Maddox's question brought another spurt of fresh tears to her eyes. She'd done her best to make him believe she could be just as hardhearted as he was, and she didn't intend to let him down. But what kind of person was she going to be once their marriage was over? Was her heart going to be nothing but a piece of stone? Or a bunch of torn, ragged pieces?

Lifting her head, she walked to the bathroom and washed the tears away with sluices of cold water. Afterward, she forced herself to smile at her image in the mirror over the vanity.

She'd promised her mother that from this day forward, she was going to be happy, and she darned well planned to keep that pledge.

Later that afternoon, at the loading dock of Bronco Feed and Ranch Supply, Maddox stood watching a forklift driver set the last pallet of feed sacks onto the flatbed trailer, when someone from behind slapped a hand on his shoulder.

"Hey, buddy. Don't tell me you're actually working today."

Recognizing Wes's voice, Maddox grinned broadly as he turned to his old running pal. "I've been known to work once in a while," he joked, then aimed a playful punch to Wes's shoulder. "Man, am I glad to see you. How's it going?"

Maddox's enthusiastic greeting pulled a chuckle from Wes. "What's all this? We just talked a few days ago. You act like we haven't seen each other in years."

Maddox shrugged. "To me it seems like years. Now that you and Evy are engaged, we don't have a chance to get together very often."

Wes didn't try to deny Maddox's observation. "It's not that I didn't enjoy those nights of making rounds at the clubs and doing our fair share of hell-raising. It was all fun. But a man's life changes when he brings a woman into things, Maddox. You'll find that out for yourself—eventually."

The forklift driver motioned to Maddox that the

last of the cattle pellets had been loaded. He gave the young man a thumbs-up, then turned back to Wes.

"I think I'm beginning to get the picture," he said to Wes, then asked, "Have you finished your business here at the feed store? If you have the time, I thought we might have a cup of coffee."

Wes said, "Dad sent me in for a few fencing supplies. As soon as those are loaded I'll meet you somewhere. Better make it Buffalo Stop. Its parking lot is big enough to accommodate our trailers."

Maddox nodded. "I'll be there."

Twenty minutes later, Maddox was sitting in a worn red vinyl booth staring thoughtfully out a plate glass window. Buffalo Stop was located on the north edge of town, next to the main highway that ran east and west away from Bronco. As usual, the traffic was full of semitrucks and trailers, but Maddox wasn't really seeing any of the passing vehicles. He was thinking about Adeline and wondering what had happened when her parents had gotten a look at her engagement ring.

So far today he hadn't heard from her. The fact irked him, although he didn't know why. It wasn't like she needed to call him just to hear his voice.

"Sorry I'm late," Wes apologized as he slipped into the seat opposite Maddox. "The workers at the feed store had a mix-up about the size of fence posts I needed."

"Don't worry about it," Maddox told him. "If you need to get on back to the Flying A, I'll understand."

Wes shook his head. "You know Dad. He's never in that big of a hurry. His motto is whatever gets done in a day's time is what gets done, and tomorrow will begin where the last one left off. So I have enough time for coffee with a friend."

Maddox gave him a wry smile. "Yeah. Lucky you, your dad is a laid-back guy."

Wes chuckled. "Yours isn't exactly a taskmaster."

"No. But he—"

Maddox broke off as a middle-aged waitress with a tired face arrived to take their order. After scribbling down two coffees and two apple pies on a notepad, she left for the kitchen.

Maddox picked up the conversation where he'd left off. "Dad can be demanding about some things."

"I imagine you're talking about the wedding thing now." Wes shook his head with wry disbelief. "After we talked the other day, Maddox, I kept thinking how ridiculous the whole situation is. It's unbelievable that your father ever conjured up the idea. And it's even more incredible that you wanted to take him up on it. I hope you've gotten the silly idea of a fake marriage out of your head."

Maddox grimaced. "You can quit hoping. That's why I wanted us to have coffee, so I'd have a chance to tell you. I'm engaged."

"Oh, hell." Wes groaned. "You've obviously lost your mind."

He'd lost something, Maddox thought, because ever since he'd slipped the diamonds onto Adeline's finger, some sort of weird switch had flipped inside him. He'd been getting the ridiculous idea that the two of them were engaged for real. It was hysterical, and yet he couldn't bring himself to utter one laugh.

The waitress arrived with their pie and coffee, and Maddox held his reply until she went on her way.

"I don't think so." He pushed back his Stetson and knocked his knuckles against his temple. "I think my mind is still up there. And going with me wherever I go."

Scowling at him, Wes said, "This isn't anything to joke about, Maddox. We're talking about your life—your happiness."

Maddox nodded. "Exactly. And that's what this marriage is going to do—make me happy."

Wes rolled his eyes. "Because it's going to give you the major share of the Double J? Believe me, Maddox, you're going to discover that land and livestock can't measure up to having a woman's love. Real love. Not the roll-in-the-hay kind."

Pulling back the reins on his temper, Maddox sliced into his pie. "Adeline is not the roll-in-the-hay kind. Like I told you on the phone the other day, she's a respectable lady."

Wes picked up his coffee cup. "Then what is she doing marrying you? It can't be for love. And just who is this Adeline who's agreed to be your wife?"

It can't be for love. No, Wes was right about that. But he wanted to think Adeline cared about him. And he cared about her.

"Adeline Longsworth. She's tall, dark-haired, beautiful and full of class. She's Louis Longsworth's daughter—he owns the Lazy L."

Wes's jaw dropped, and his cup stopped halfway to his mouth. "Oh, brother! You've really stepped in it, haven't you?"

Maddox glanced around the interior of the little café to make sure no one was listening, then, for a safety measure, he leaned slightly toward Wes. "What the heck is that supposed to mean?" he asked in a hushed voice. "Did you expect me to just grab any woman off the street? Mom and Dad would've seen right through the whole sham."

Wes's short laugh was nothing but mockery. "You're delusional if you think your parents won't eventually see through this. And when that happens, you can kiss anything you might've inherited good-bye. Nobody likes a cheater or a liar, and that's how Randall is going to see you."

Wes had been his best buddy for years, and Maddox didn't want to get angry with the guy. But the more Wes talked, the more Maddox felt his back teeth grinding together.

"Wes, do you remember when you got peeved with me when I tried to talk you out of dating Evy? You told me to get out of your face. Now you're trying to get in mine, and I'm not sure I like it."

"Yeah, I remember. I got peeved with you because I was falling in love with Evy—for real."

Maddox smirked. "And you think that makes my

engagement any less important than yours? People marry for all kinds of reasons, and most of those reasons have nothing to do with love."

"Is that what you're telling yourself?" Carefully eyeing Maddox, he leaned back in the booth and reached for his coffee. "You know, I'm beginning to think that you're getting all bristled at me because you're actually falling for Miss Adeline Longsworth."

Maddox's mouth flopped open. "Don't be stupid," he finally managed to say. "You might want to live a caged life, but not me. Once Dad signs the major share of the ranch over to me, the marriage ends. I'll be free as a mustang again."

Wes pointed his fork at Maddox's plate. "Better enjoy your pie, Maddox. 'Cause sooner or later you're going to be eating crow."

During the next few days, Louis Longsworth remained steadfast in his feelings about his daughter's engagement. He'd made it clear to her and anyone who cared to listen—if Maddox stepped one foot onto Lazy L property, Louis would take pleasure in throwing him off. And if he couldn't physically manage the feat, he'd call the law and have a deputy do it for him.

Surprisingly, Adeline had held her temper and stuck to her plan to remain on a happy, positive keel. She'd not argued, pleaded or attempted in any way to defend her decisions to her father. After all, there was nothing he could do to stop her from marrying Maddox. And, at this point, becoming Maddox's wife was all that mattered to her.

As for Maddox, he wasn't the least bit pleased when she'd told him about Louis's threats. Especially when it meant he couldn't drive out to the Lazy L to pick up Adeline for a date or simply visit her. If they met for any reason, Adeline had to go to him.

Although Adeline hadn't known Maddox for very long, it was clear to her that he was a man who didn't want to back away from any obstacle. And that included her father. As far as Maddox was concerned, Louis was too much of a coward to meet his future son-in-law. But thankfully, for her sake, he'd promised to keep his distance from Louis. How that was going to work once she and Maddox were actually married, she had no clue.

But this evening, Adeline wasn't going to worry about the problem with her father. The Bronco Harvest Festival was in full swing, and she was meeting Maddox so the two of them could enjoy the festivities together.

The bulk of the festival took place at the Bronco Fairgrounds, but the businesses in town also took advantage of the influx of people. Many of them offered sidewalk sales and free hot chocolate and apple cider.

Traffic was heavy as Adeline drove into town, and as she maneuvered her way down one of the main thoroughfares, she noticed groups of people were gathered up and down the sidewalks.

Maddox had promised he'd be waiting for her at the Bronco Ghost Tours building with a few of his friends. When she reached the street where it was located, she discovered every parking space was already filled. After a futile search for a vacant spot, she decided to park in the alley and walk around to the ghost tour building.

Even though the sun hadn't yet sunk behind the distant mountains, the air had grown chilly. As she made her way to the end of the block, then down the sidewalk toward Bronco Ghost Tours, she was glad she'd worn a knit scarf and gloves with her shearling and denim jacket. Yet the chilly evening certainly hadn't put a damper on the town's celebration.

Conversation and laughter buzzed as people shopped the wares displayed out on the sidewalk. Children dashed about carrying sacks of candy and goodies, and as Adeline passed a small antique shop, an elderly lady pressed a foam cup filled with hot chocolate into her hand.

Smiling cheerily, the woman said, "Happy harvest!"

"Yes. Thank you," she told her, then added with a little wave, "Same to you."

Adeline continued walking on down the sidewalk while carefully sipping the drink and trying not to spill it as she jostled her way through the crowd.

"Adeline! Over here!"

Recognizing Maddox's voice, she stood on her tiptoes and searched for a sign of his particular black hat among the dozens of other cowboy hats being worn in the group of people milling about on the sidewalk. After a moment, she spotted him, along with Jameson and Vanessa, standing a short distance away.

Waving to him, she worked her way over to the group, but before she could say hello to anyone, Maddox swept her into his arms and placed a long, warm kiss on her lips.

Her first instinct was to cling to him and urge him to keep the kiss going. But they had an audience, and besides, she wasn't supposed to actually be wanting his kiss. She was only supposed to pretend she wanted his kiss.

Behind her, Jameson cleared his throat. "Uh, Maddox, you're in a public place—with kids around."

Easing Adeline out of his arms, Maddox laughed at his brother while Vanessa gouged an elbow in Jameson's rib cage. "Don't be such a fuddy-duddy, Jameson. Adeline and Maddox are in love and newly engaged. Why shouldn't they show their affection?"

"Yeah, big brother," Maddox said with a playful grin. "Maybe you should start showing Van a little more PDA."

While Jameson ignored the remark, Maddox slipped an arm around Adeline's waist and urged her toward a tall cowboy and a pretty young brunette standing a few short steps away. The cowboy was holding an adorable little girl with blond curls, who appeared to be around two years old.

"Adeline, meet Tyler Abernathy and his fiancée, Callie Sheldrick. And the sweet little angel in her daddy's arms is Maeve," he introduced the trio to Adeline.

"I'm happy to meet you all." Adeline started to shake hands and then realized she was still clutching the cup of cocoa. "Sorry. My drink has gone cold. I need to toss it."

"Here. Let me, sweetheart." Maddox took the cup from her and dropped it into a nearby trash barrel.

Sweetheart? Nice touch of acting on his part, Adeline thought as she shook hands with Tyler and Callie. Maddox had probably used the same endearment for every girlfriend he'd ever had dated. But she doubted he'd ever considered the meaning behind the word.

Back at her side, Maddox explained to his friends, "Adeline is a Longsworth. Her folks own the Lazy L. I'm sure you're familiar with the spread."

"Sure. It's one of the biggest ranches in this part of the state," Tyler said, then grinned at Adeline. "My brother Wes told us that Maddox had gotten engaged. So you're the woman who's lassoed his heart. Congratulations. It's a pleasure to meet you, Adeline."

"Yes, congratulations," Callie added, her gaze going straight to Adeline's left hand. "Are you wearing your ring? I'd love to see it."

Maddox was quick to joke, "After the fortune I spent on it, she'd better be wearing it!"

Casting Maddox a meaningful glanced, Adeline pulled the glove from her hand and held it out toward the couple.

Callie took a closer look at the diamonds, "Oh my. If Maddox picked this out himself, you must have been stunned when you saw it."

"He did choose the ring," Adeline told her. "And I admit I was a bit speechless when I saw it."

Tyler said, "Maddox, you certainly didn't hold back when you went to the jewelers. After seeing Adeline's ring, Callie is going to want have more diamonds added to hers."

Callie smiled up at her fiancé. "I'm perfectly satisfied with my ring. And you."

Maddox glanced at Adeline, and she could have sworn there was a look of pride on his face.

He said to Tyler, "When a woman plans to wear a ring for the rest of her life, a man better make sure she's happy with it."

It was all Adeline could do to keep from rolling her eyes. Sure, he wanted everyone to believe he was madly in love with her. But this talk about the rest of her life was totally unnecessary, she thought. More than that, it was only going to make them both look worse when they suddenly divorced.

Callie cast Adeline an understanding smile. "Have you gotten used to being engaged yet? Honestly, it took a week or more before the whole idea sank in on me."

"To tell you the truth, I'm still a little dazed,"

Adeline told her. Which was certainly true. She'd gone from meeting Maddox one night to agreeing to become his wife the next afternoon. She felt as if she was riding a runaway horse without any reins!

"She's dazed because she's so wild about me," Maddox teased as his hand gently squeezed the side of her waist.

Prompted by his touch, she looked up and gave him an adoring smile. "That's the only reason I'm marrying you, sweetheart. Because I'm totally wild about you."

One of his brows arched faintly, and then the corner of his mouth crooked slightly upward. "I should explain that Tyler's older brother, Wes, has been my good friend for years. I told him about our engagement."

Nodding, she looked at Tyler. "I think I remember seeing you and your brothers at the Fourth of July celebration here in town. You were selling cuts of beef at one of the booths. Are you related to the Abernathys who own the Ambling A Ranch?"

"Yes. George Abernathy is my uncle. So we have a heap of relatives in the area."

"What Tyler is actually saying, Adeline, is that by the time he explained how he was related to all the Abernathys around Bronco, all the festivities would be shut down for the night," Jameson said.

"Say, what is this, a family reunion?"

Adeline looked around to see the question had come from a dark-haired man around Maddox's age.

Since he was releasing his hold on the glass door leading into the ghost tour office, she assumed he must have just exited the place.

"Sort of," Callie told him. "We're getting to know Adeline, Maddox's fiancée."

Maddox quickly introduced her to Evan Cruise, owner of Bronco Ghost Tours.

"Evan is Callie's boss," Vanessa explained with a heartfelt smile at Callie. "Although she's the one who keeps the place running smoothly."

"That's true enough," Evan said with a little laugh. "Callie is quite a salesperson. She can talk the most skeptical person into going on a ghost tour."

"So where's your better half, Evan?" Maddox asked. "Isn't she going to join in the fun of the festival?"

"Are you kidding?" Evan said. "When a crowd comes to town, Daphne takes full advantage of it. She's out at the fairgrounds. You'll find her as soon as you go through the gates. That's where she's set up her Happy Hearts petting zoo. Next to it she's erected a pen for the animals that are available for adoption."

Recognizing the Happy Hearts name, Adeline looked at him with interest. "Daphne, the owner of Happy Hearts Animal Sanctuary, is your wife?"

Evan's grin was a picture of pride. "The one and only. Do you know her?"

Adeline nodded. "I go out to Happy Hearts every now and then to make a donation. Being a rancher's daughter, I'm well aware of the huge amount of funding it takes to care for animals. Your wife needs all the help she can get."

"And let me guess," Evan said with wry amusement. "You give it to her without your father knowing."

Surprised by the man's comments, Adeline asked, "How did you know?"

He shrugged. "Most of the ranchers around here don't approve of my wife's ideas of saving animals they raise for slaughter."

She said, "Well, I'm glad to know my father isn't the only narrow-minded rancher in these parts. But that doesn't stop me from helping Daphne's orphaned animals."

Maddox looked at her. "I didn't know you were such an animal lover."

She gave him another sweet and pointed smile. "There are still lots of things you haven't learned about me yet."

She felt his fingers subtly tighten at her waist. "Obviously," he said then glanced at Evan. "I imagine you've been trying to think up a way to capitalize on this excitement over Bobby Stone's ghost. Have you come up with some sort of tour about him yet?"

"I'm planning to work up something," Evan said. "Only I need more information first."

Adeline cast a curious look around the group. "I've been seeing all kind of flyers around town asking if anyone has seen Bobby Stone. Who is he? I thought he was a real person—not a ghost!"

"None of us actually knew him personally," Callie replied. "He used to live in Bronco, but he supposedly died."

"Supposedly?" Adeline questioned.

"Some folks are reporting they've seen the man alive and right here in Bronco," Vanessa answered, then grinned at Evan. "Perfect fodder for my brother, who loves a good ghost story."

Adeline frowned with confusion. "I don't understand."

"Well, the story goes that Bobby sat on the haunted stool at Doug's bar."

"What is the haunted stool?" Adeline wanted to know.

"They call it the 'Death Seat' because it presumably causes bad things to happen to a person who sits in it. Well, after Bobby left the bar, he went for a hike up in the mountains just outside of Bronco and fell off a ledge and into a deep ravine. Rescuers found his belongings on the cliff, but Bobby's body was never found. The area was searched, but no sign of him was ever found. The steepness of the gorge, plus the dense brush probably didn't help."

"How awful," Adeline remarked. "I suppose some folks blame the haunted stool for his death."

"They do," Evan replied. "But in Bobby's case, many think he was drunk and simply lost his footing."

They discussed the Bobby Stone subject a few more minutes before Maddox said, "I think Adeline and I will mosey on out to the festival. Do any of you need a ride?"

Everyone assured him they'd be driving out to the fairgrounds later on, and Maddox wasted no time hustling her away from his friends and down the busy sidewalk.

When they reached the end of the block, she shot him a bewildered look. "Am I wrong, or are you in a hurry?"

With his hand on her arm, he guided her around the corner and down an adjoining sidewalk. When they reached a spot where they were partially out of view from the bulk of the crowd, he yanked her toward him.

"Damn right I'm in a hurry," he said. "To do this."

Adeline barely had time to look up before his lips came down on hers.

The kiss wasn't gentle. It was hot and hungry and left her in a breathless huff.

"What's the matter with you?" she demanded. "We don't have an audience now. There's no need for you to keep acting."

His short, self-deprecating laugh confused her as much as his kiss.

"I wasn't acting. I was investigating. I wanted to find out if you're the same woman I became engaged to a few days ago."

Skeptical of his explanation, she asked, "Am I the same woman?"

"I'm not sure." His lips took on a wry twist. "Not sure at all."

All of a sudden, her heart was tapping a rapid rhythm against her breast, and try as she might, she couldn't stop her gaze from zeroing in on his lips. "Having buyer's remorse?" she asked.

His hand glided up and down her upper arm, and in spite of her thick jacket, the touch warmed her flesh.

"Quite the opposite, Adeline. I'm thinking it's going to be tons of fun having you as my pretend wife."

Fun? After that kiss? No, it was going to be dangerous, she decided. For the both of them.

Chapter Eight

During the short ride to the Bronco Fairgrounds, Maddox wondered who the hell he was trying to fool. Adeline or himself? The excuse he'd given her for hustling her away from his friends and kissing her as if there would be no tomorrow had been stupid. His behavior had been stupid. But something had come over him while the two of them had been standing there talking and interacting with his friends. All of a sudden, he'd desperately needed to kiss her, to hold her and reassure himself that, at least for the moment, she was *his* woman.

And that wasn't a part of the bargain he'd made with her. It wasn't even a part of the bargain he'd made with himself. Now what was she thinking?

That he needed her to be more than a fake wife to him? No. He had to stop doing or saying things that might give her the wrong ideas. He had to get a grip on himself. Before this whole scheme blew up in his face.

"Maddox, is anything wrong? If you'd rather not do the Harvest Festival, that's okay with me. We can do something else. Go somewhere quieter," she suggested.

Groaning inwardly, he glanced over at her. He'd never been too good at resisting temptation, so being in a quiet place, alone with Adeline, would be the height of enticement.

"Nothing is wrong, Adeline. I'm looking forward to the festival," he told her.

"I wasn't sure. You've seemed a bit preoccupied ever since we left town."

He forced a smile on his face. "Just thinking about what we should do first—play games or eat. And by the way, those boots are kick-ass cute on you."

She looked down at the new pair of cowboy boots she'd purchased specifically to wear this weekend. "Thanks. I like them, too," she said, then gave him an impish smile. "Did you notice I'm in a regular denim jacket lined with shearling? No fancy faux fur."

"You look just right," he told her. Actually, she looked like a dream, Maddox thought. But he kept that fact to himself as he steered his truck off the highway and into a wide parking area where local law enforcement was directing a steady stream of arriving vehicles.

After parking in a designated spot, they walked through the maze of parked vehicles until they reached the main entrance, where crowds of people were already making their way through the open gates.

Maddox reached for Adeline's hand. "I don't want to lose you in the crowd," he explained, feeling the need to give her a reason for the hold he had on her hand.

The smile she gave him was genuine. "If we got separated in this throng of people, I'd probably never find you. I don't remember the festival being this large. Has it grown in the past two years, or am I imagining things?"

He shot her a sheepish look. "I don't know," he admitted. "I haven't been out here in— Well, let's just say it's been a long time."

She laughed. "Uh-huh. Who was the guy who kept insisting he was pure hayseed?"

He chuckled with her. "Okay. So I lost interest in pumpkin growing and horseshoe pitching. But that doesn't mean I can't get into the swing of it again."

"Right. Well, let's see if we can find something to catch your interest."

At the moment, his interest was on the way the lights were glistening on the dark, silky hair lying against her shoulders and the way her brown eyes were soft and warm each time they met his. It was nice being with her, he thought. Too nice, in fact.

"Oh, look, Maddox," she said, while tugging on his hand. "Just like Evan told us. There's the Happy Hearts petting zoo and adoption booth. Let's go look."

They walked over to the fenced-off enclosure Daphne had set up for the animals needing permanent homes. Near one section of the portable fence, several wire crates held cats of all different sizes and colors. On the opposite side, an assortment of dogs yelped and barked for attention. Adeline gave them a passing glance before heading straight to the felines.

"Aw, Maddox, aren't they beautiful?" Bending at the waist, she poked her finger through a hole in the fence in an effort to catch the attention of a black-and-white kitten.

"You like cats?" Maddox asked.

"I love cats. But Mom is allergic to them, so I can't have one in the house. There are several barn cats on the ranch, to keep down the rat population, but they're mostly wild." Twisting her head around, she gave him a resigned smile. "What about you? I imagine you're a dog guy, right?"

"Well, dogs on the Double J are considered ranch hands. So they're my work buddies. But I like cats. Mom has two house cats, and sometimes they sleep with me."

Straightening to her full height, she turned to him. "You're lucky, Maddox. In more ways than you realize."

Yes, he was a fortunate guy. Funny that it had taken Adeline to remind him of all his blessings.

"Yeah, I guess I am. I'll tell you something else, Adeline. Once you and I are married, you can have all the cats you want."

She squeezed his hand, but the joy he expected to see flash in her eyes never appeared. "That's nice of you, Maddox. But I wouldn't want to get a cat. I'd get attached to the animal, and then when you and I divorced, I'd probably have to give it up. Finding an apartment that allows pets isn't always easy. And giving up the cat—well, I wouldn't want to go through that."

He felt sick, although he wasn't exactly sure why. Was it the word *divorce* that had put a rock in the pit of his stomach? Or was it the idea of her moving on and away from him?

"Sorry. I wasn't thinking that far ahead." Placing a hand against the small of her back, he said, "Let's see what else the festival has to offer."

"I'm ready." She lifted her nose to the air. "In fact, I'm getting whiffs of funnel cakes. I'd love one with some hot coffee. What about you?"

"Sounds good to me. We'll follow your nose," he told her.

They moved into the carnival-like atmosphere, where music was playing and people of all ages were milling from one attraction to the next. Most folks were carrying food or drinks in their hands, while many of the children toted stuffed animals and clutched long strings with balloons flying on the ends.

After finding the booth selling the funnel cakes, Maddox purchased two of the sweet treats, both coated in powdered sugar and large enough to cover the entire paper plate. To one side of the food vendor van, a canvas canopy was erected over a cluster of small utility tables. Most of them were occupied, but they found one where most of the cold wind was blocked by the van.

Once they'd finished their cakes and coffee, they walked through the throngs of festivalgoers, past endless booths displaying arts and crafts for sale, and all types of games to test a person's skills, along with dozens more fast-food options.

Eventually, Maddox tried his hand at hitting a moving target with a baseball, and after three attempts, he managed to win his choice of stuffed animals.

"I'll take the yellow tabby cat. He looks like he needs a home," Maddox told the bony-faced older man overseeing the game.

"Not much to that one," the man said. "You can have any of the larger toys if you want."

"The tabby will do," Maddox assured him.

He handed the toy to Maddox, who, in turn, presented the little trophy to Adeline. "For you," he told her. "He can be a stand-in for a real cat. You don't even have to bother with food or a litter box."

"Thank you, Maddox. He's cute." She cuddled the toy in the crook of her arm but didn't reward him with a smile.

Her lackluster reaction had Maddox second-guessing his choice of toys. Maybe he should have taken one of the teddy bears or the grinning monkey, anything but a damned cat, he thought.

But just as quickly, he recognized, he was thinking like an idiot. It wasn't his place to make Adeline smile. Being her fake fiancé didn't mean he had a responsibility to make her happy.

Annoyed with his thoughts, he guided her away from the baseball toss and on toward a field where mounds of pumpkins were illuminated by stadium-type lights.

"Are you up to trying the hayride?" he asked as they strolled along a footpath at the edge of the field. "It's getting cold. If you're not comfortable, we can call it a night."

"I'm warm enough. And I've always liked the hayride. My sister and I used to take the tour together."

He glanced at her. "I'll be honest, when you first told me you had attended the Harvest Festival, I didn't much believe you."

She looked surprised. "Why would you think that? It's an annual Bronco tradition, and all kinds of people attend."

"True. But I didn't think this type of entertainment was your thing. I mean, you're more of a night-at-the-ballet kind of girl."

"Like tutus and slippers instead of cowboy boots and jeans?" She chuckled softly. "Boy, do I ever have you fooled. What you see is just an image. I'm a country girl at heart."

He chuckled. "Who happens to like designer things in her closet."

"I do. But none of that is what makes me be me." She pulled an impish face at him. "Besides, I've been having the same thoughts about you. You're not a pumpkin-patch kind of guy. You're more of a cold-beer-and-a-game-of-pool type."

He gave her a guilty grin. "So we've veered out of our elements tonight. We're having fun anyway, aren't we?"

She looped her arm through his and snuggled closer to his side. "Loads of fun."

When they reached the spot where the hayrides started and ended, Maddox purchased two tickets and handed them to a young man overseeing the loading and unloading of passengers.

"It'll be another ten minutes before the wagon returns." The man gestured to a few wooden benches located to their left. "You can wait over there if you'd like."

By now, a north wind had started to sweep across the fairgrounds, and when Adeline looked up at the sky, she noticed clouds had moved in to cover the stars.

"It's getting colder." She pulled the red sock cap she was wearing farther down over her ears. "I wouldn't be surprised to see snow falling before the night is over."

He curved his arm around her shoulders and tugged her closer to his side. "Hmm. Might be nice to take a hayride in the snow," he murmured. "It would give us something to tell our grandchildren."

She looked at him. He wasn't making sense—or perhaps she was reading more into his comment than what was actually behind it. "Well, yes. I suppose kids would enjoy hearing about a hayride. Except that our grandchildren won't be related."

His eyes widened as though that reality had never entered his head, and she could only think he'd taken his acting skills to an even higher level.

"Oh. Yeah. I keep forgetting. We're not going to have a real marriage."

She shook her head. "How could you possibly forget such an important part of our deal?"

A faint smile tugged at the corners of his lips. "Must be all this rehearsing and acting we've been doing. Makes it hard to hold on to reality."

He'd certainly been doing his part of holding on, she decided, as the hand on her upper arm continued to clasp her tightly to his side. But she could honestly say she didn't mind. In fact, she was beginning to like it. Far, far too much.

"Do you think this round of public appearances is doing any good in making folks around here believe our engagement?" she asked. "So far I haven't spotted anyone I know."

"I have. When we were making our way through the vendors, I noticed some of my parents' friends eyeing us. So you can bet they'll be spreading the word. Besides, you've gotten a cat from this outing." He inclined his head toward the toy jammed beneath her arm. "What are you going to name him?"

She thought for a moment. "I believe I'll call him Festus."

A comical frown wrinkled his features. "Are you kidding? What happened to Felix? Isn't that a typical name for a male cat?"

"This one isn't typical. And for your information, Festus is a name of Latin origin meaning 'festive.' Get it? Festive—festival—Festus?"

He laughed loudly enough to turn a few heads in their direction. "Oh, Adeline, you are way over my head."

"Okay," she said with a guilty grin. "I confess. I don't know Latin. I only knew all that because I had an uncle named Festus, and he took great pleasure in explaining the origin of his name."

"Ha! And here I was thinking you were exceptionally smart. And I also had the feeling you didn't like your little cat."

She frowned at him. "You shouldn't think so much, Maddox. You might get hurt."

Before he could make a reply, the big green farm tractor pulling the hay wagon rolled to a stop a short distance from where they were sitting. As the passengers departed, Adeline and Maddox rose from the bench and stood in an out-of-the-way spot until it was time for them to follow the new group onto the flatbed trailer.

The bale of hay Maddox chose for them to sit on was located at the tail end of the trailer. Adeline didn't question his choice, but after the wagon began to move, she realized the position was better because they wouldn't have to peer over or around the heads of other passengers.

"Who are you looking for back there, Adeline? Bobby Stone? I doubt you'll find his ghost riding along with us tonight."

She looked away from the group of people seated behind them and pulled a playful face at him. "I wouldn't know Bobby Stone if I met him on the street—in person or as a ghost. But now that you brought him up, we are getting closer to Halloween. It would be kind of neat to think a ghost was taking this hayride with us."

He feigned a shiver. "Sweetheart, don't say that. You're spooking me," he joked.

"I doubt you've ever been spooked," she told him. "Unless it was when you were a little boy."

"Mom says as a kid I was never afraid of anything. Even the things I should've been afraid of. I don't know how true that is. But I can tell you that I haven't taken a hayride since I was young teenager," Maddox said. "Nowadays, the only time I'm on a trailer load of hay is when we're stacking the bales in the loft of the barn."

He had cuddled her so close to his side she had to tilt her head back in order to look at his face. The faint smile she saw on his lips hinted at fond memories.

"It's good that Randall has sons to help him work the ranch and keep it thriving," she said. "I often think Dad might have been a different person if Emily and I had been sons instead of daughters."

His blue eyes shifted to her face. "Plenty of women do ranch work. Some even own and run their own ranches. You and your sister were never interested in getting involved with working the Lazy L?"

She grimaced. "You might not believe this, but Emily and I both wanted to be a part of the running of the ranch. It was our home, and we both loved animals and the outdoors."

"I'm sorry, Adeline. But that's hard to believe. I mean, I've never met your sister, but if she's anything like you— Well, you don't look anything close to the outdoor type."

She sighed and looked away from him. Currently, the wagon was moving past the huge pumpkin patch, but she wasn't exactly seeing the mounds of orange fruit. Instead she was seeing herself and Emily as young girls, begging their father to let them go on spring roundup. He'd been horrified that they'd even approached him with such an idea.

She said, "You're right, Maddox. No one would guess that Emily and I would have ever wanted to feed an orphaned calf a bottle or spread grain in feed troughs. But we did want to. Only our father made sure we got those ideas out of our minds. You see, he's old-school. He believes the only place a woman should get her hands dirty is in the kitchen. And, too, he wanted his daughters to be like princesses—always dressed to kill and looking like we just stepped out of a salon. He thinks— Well, he's proud of our image."

"You know I don't exactly feel benevolent toward Louis Longsworth, so my opinion is obviously biased. But it sounds to me like he's tried to control you all your life."

Not only her, but also her mother and sister, Adeline could have told him. But she didn't want to point that out to Maddox tonight. And in the end, what did it really matter what Maddox thought of her father? Louis was only going to be his temporary father-in-law.

"Dad is still trying to control us. But thanks to you, Maddox, that's coming to an end for me, at least."

"Thanks to me?"

She turned her face back toward his. "Yes, you. I'll soon be Mrs. Maddox John."

His gaze connected with hers. "Mrs. Maddox John," he murmured, as though the idea still hadn't entirely registered in his brain. "I guess I am helping you out. And you're helping me out."

"Yes. We're helping each other." She looked away from him just in time to see they were passing a stretch of glistening water. "There's the lake, Maddox. And is that snow I see falling?"

"I believe you're right."

Tilting her face to the sky, she laughed softly as a few flakes splattered onto her cheeks. "This is lovely. Snow on a hayride!"

"This truly will be something to tell our grandchildren." His thumb and forefinger wrapped around her chin and pulled her face around to his. "Better let me take care of those snowflakes or you're going to have frostbite on your nose and lips."

He didn't give her a chance to wipe the flecks of snow from her face. The next thing she knew, he was kissing the tip of her nose, and then his lips settled over hers in a warm, gentle foray that built a fire deep in her belly.

No. Oh, no. This wasn't supposed to be happening. She wasn't supposed to want this man. Yet even as the wild thoughts raced through her head, her arms were slipping around his neck.

If the wagon hadn't hit a bump in the road, the kiss might have kept going. But it jostled them just enough to part their lips and let Adeline gulp in a breath of sanity.

"This is nice," he murmured. "I'm much warmer with your arms around me."

She quickly unwound them from his neck and attempted to put some space between their hips and thighs, but the arm he had around her waist held her firmly to his side.

"I realize we have to put on an act, Maddox," she primly, "but we don't know any of these people sitting behind us."

He chuckled under his breath. "Who cares if we know them, Adeline? Practice makes perfect."

The amusement she heard in his voice reminded Adeline that this was all just a game to him. He didn't have a clue that he was affecting her in a deep and irrevocable way. And she had no intention of letting Maddox discover that Louis Longsworth's princess was really just a little fool.

Chapter Nine

The next evening, Maddox was walking to his truck when Jameson intercepted him. He'd not seen his brother on the ranch today, and at lunch Mimi had remarked that Jameson and Vanessa were finally beginning to make wedding plans. As to what kind of plans, his mother hadn't elaborated, and Maddox had refrained from asking. The last thing he wanted to do was make himself appear overly interested in his brother's wedding. He could only hope that Vanessa remained steadfast in her wish for a small ceremony.

"Look at you all dressed up," Jameson commented as he eyed Maddox's dark jeans and black leather jacket. "You must be going to the harvest dance."

Maddox playfully tipped his black hat at his

brother. "You guessed it. A live band. Free refreshments. And most importantly, my beautiful fiancée to dance with me. I wouldn't miss the dance for any reason."

Jameson glanced at his watch. "I imagine it's more than a half hour from here to the Lazy L. You're going to be late."

Maddox shook his head. "I'm not going to pick up Adeline on the Lazy L. She's meeting me in town."

Jameson frowned at him. "Man, I thought you were more of a gentleman than that, little brother. What's the matter? You don't want to buy the gas it takes to drive to the Lazy L?"

For some reason, Maddox found it difficult to meet Jameson's prying gaze. "Don't be flip," he said, then scuffed the ground with the toe of his boot. "Actually, Jameson, Adeline doesn't want me coming over there yet. You see, her father is still holding a grudge against us Johns. Or that's part of the problem, I think. The other part is that he's dead set against Adeline marrying me."

Maddox expected Jameson to look surprised at the revelation, but he didn't.

He said, "Maybe Louis Longsworth doesn't believe you're marrying Adeline for the right reasons."

"I'm not sure the old codger would know the *right* reasons," Maddox muttered.

Actually, he wasn't sure Jameson knew the exact reason he was marrying Adeline. His brother might be guessing it was for the inheritance of the Double

J, but he clearly wasn't certain. And Maddox hoped neither he nor any of his family ever uncovered the truth of the matter.

"Hmm. Have you considered going over there and confronting Louis? Forcing him to talk it out with you?"

"That's exactly what I'd like to do," Maddox answered. "But Adeline has begged me to keep my distance for now. And for her sake, I've agreed."

"Sounds like you and your father-in-law are going to be great pals," Jameson said dryly.

Maddox tried not to bristle. "Not all families are perfect. Besides, I'm not marrying Louis Longsworth. I'm marrying Adeline."

Hanging his thumbs over the pockets of his jeans, Jameson rocked back on his heels and continued to regard Maddox with narrowed eyes. "How long are you going to keep up this charade?"

Just hearing Jameson refer to his engagement as a charade was worse than sticking the flame of a blowtorch to his bare skin. "What are you talking about?"

Jameson snorted. "This ridiculous notion that you're going to get married. Those huge rocks you put on Adeline's finger might fool some people, but not me. I'm your brother, remember? I know how your mind works. You wouldn't recognize love if it slapped you in the face. This is all about the ranch and you trying to grab your share. Or what you regard as your share."

Now that Jameson had brought up the elephant in

the room, Maddox lost what little grip he had on his temper. Anger flashed through him like lightning hitting dry prairie grass.

"*Your* share," Maddox sneered. "That's something you don't have to worry about, is it? No. Hierarchy is easy to come by. It doesn't require skill, or work ethic. It's just handed to you—like a gift."

"Maddox, you're way off base, and—"

"No, you're the one who's way off base here, Jameson. My engagement to Adeline isn't a charade! We truly are getting married, and soon! So think on that!"

Jameson's jaw dropped, but Maddox didn't wait around to see what sort of reply his brother was going to fire back at him. He stalked off, his long, angry strides quickly carrying him to his truck.

He was driving away from the ranch yard before he dared to glance in the side mirror. Jameson was still standing where he'd left him, and Maddox could only wonder what was going through his brother's mind. Did he plan to tell their father about their heated exchange?

If Jameson ended up being a snitch, it wouldn't garner him any points, Maddox thought hotly. Maddox was the son who was going to give their parents what they wanted the most—a wedding big enough to give the Johns bragging rights among their rich friends.

He'd driven halfway to Bronco before his temper cooled and his thoughts turned to the evening ahead. He was looking forward to seeing Adeline again. When he was with her, everything around him seemed softer and easier. And not just because she was helping him achieve a goal. For the first time in his life, he felt as if someone actually needed him, and, foolish or not, he wanted to hold on to that heady sensation.

He hadn't expected to enjoy attending the Harvest Festival last night. Yet he'd ended up not wanting the evening to end. And even after he'd said good night to Adeline and driven home, he hadn't been able to get her out of his mind.

Kissing her was just as risky as playing with fire. But he'd always enjoyed flirting with danger, and besides, he wasn't touching Adeline with serious thoughts in his head. Getting serious wasn't a part of their deal.

It would give us something to tell our grandchildren.

Maddox didn't know why he'd made such a slip of the tongue. The words had simply spilled out of him. And she'd responded with such a weird look on her face that he'd felt like a complete idiot.

Imagine him, a certified bachelor, with children, much less grandchildren. It was laughable. So why hadn't Adeline laughed? More importantly, why hadn't Maddox laughed? The answer to those questions was something he didn't want to think about.

Fortunately, the few snowflakes that had floated through the air the night before had quickly dissipated, and this evening the temperature was much warmer, making it perfect for the Harvest Festival dance.

An open area of Bronco City Park had been roped off, and a large portable floor had been erected for dancing. Strings of lights fashioned like mini jack-o'-lanterns were strung across the wide expanse of wooden floor, while outside the dance area, hay bales flanked with pots of gold and orange mums provided seating for couples who might need a breather.

Throughout the park, wispy white cobwebs, along with ghosts and skeletons, hung from tree limbs, while long utility tables offering refreshments were situated near a stand of cedar trees. At the far west end of the dance floor, a five-piece band positioned on a small elevated platform had begun to play, filling the night air with country music.

Dressed in a tiered maxi dress of tiny orange and green flowers printed on broadcloth, Adeline stood at the edge of the crowd. As she tapped the toe of her boot to the country music, she glanced over at Trudy, who'd managed to change her shift at the hospital in order to attend the dance with her date.

"Looks like the crowd is going to be huge tonight," Adeline commented. "Most of Bronco has turned out for this event. And it's great that you got to come with Vincent tonight. I can tell he likes you, Trudy. A lot. And he seems like a stand-up guy."

Trudy blushed at the mention of the EMT, who'd left her side a couple of minutes ago to fetch cups of punch from the refreshment table. Her friend had been hoping for months that Vincent would ask her for a date. Now that it had finally happened, Adeline couldn't have been happier for her.

"He is a stand-up guy, Adeline," she said with a fond smile. "Just like your fiancé is a stand-up guy. And, by the way, where is he? Isn't it about time Maddox showed up?"

Trudy had barely had time to get the words out of her mouth before Maddox walked up behind Adeline and slipped his arms around her waist.

Twisting around in his arms, she exclaimed, "There you are! I was beginning to think you were going to stand me up."

"Fat chance of that happening." He lowered his head and placed a kiss on her lips before he turned his attention to Trudy. "Have we met? I think I've seen you before."

Trudy nodded. "I came in to DJ's Deluxe one night when you and Adeline were having a drink together at the bar."

"Oh, yes, I remember." He looked at Adeline and winked. "Had to be one of the best nights of my life."

A calculating look came over Trudy's face, and Adeline quickly cleared her throat and introduced the two of them properly.

Maddox had just shaken hands with her when Vincent, a tall man in his thirties with wavy black hair, strolled up with the punch cups in hand. Adeline wasted no time in introducing the two men, and surprisingly, they both appeared to remember each other.

"Yeah, you're the EMT guy," Maddox told him. "You came out to the Double J with the ambulance when one of the ranch hands took a bad spill from a horse. We were afraid he'd broken his back."

Vincent nodded. "Sure, I remember. You saved him from a worse injury by not moving him. How's he doing now?"

"Great. He had to lay off work for a while. But he's back in full swing now."

The two were still discussing Vincent's job when Maddox's younger brother, Dawson, walked up. Maddox promptly introduced him to Adeline and after he'd greeted her and the rest of the group, he asked, "Have any of you heard the rumor yet?"

"What rumor? That you couldn't get a date tonight?" Maddox teased.

"Not hardly," he said with a smirk for his brother. "I wanted to come stag so I could dance with all the pretty girls."

Maddox groaned, and Adeline asked, "Is there really some rumor going around?"

Dawson nodded. "People have been saying that Bobby Stone is going to make an appearance at the dance tonight."

"Oh brother," Maddox said drolly. "And here I thought you might have something really juicy to tell us. Everyone knows Bobby Stone is dead. If he makes an appearance, this park will empty so fast, it'll whip what's left of the leaves off the trees."

Dawson rolled his eyes at his brother. "I'm not talking about a ghost! A few folks are swearing they've actually seen the man in the flesh—walking around Bronco. Probably because Halloween is coming. Come to think of it, it'd be the perfect occasion for a ghost to make an appearance."

Except for Adeline, everyone in the group scoffed at Dawson's idea, and the subject was dropped until Maddox led her onto the dance floor.

After he'd pulled her into his arms and moved them in step with the music, he asked, "I noticed you didn't dismiss Dawson's remarks about Bobby Stone. Do you believe the man's ghost is actually walking around Bronco?"

She turned her face toward his and discovered the space between their lips was so scant their breaths were mingling. The close proximity, coupled with the sensation of his strong arm wrapped around her waist, made her wish she had a legitimate reason to kiss him.

"I wouldn't go so far as to say his ghost is going around town. I'd rather believe it's someone who resembles this man. That makes more sense, doesn't it?"

He smiled just enough to flash a bit of white teeth. Adeline drew in a deep breath and tried not to think how it might feel to have those teeth gently nibbling on her neck, her breasts—any and everywhere he wanted.

He said, "Yes. But common sense isn't nearly as fun as the idea of being visited by a ghost. Just ask Evan. He makes a living off spooking people with ghoulish stories."

"He certainly needs to take advantage of the Bobby Stone legend," Adeline said. "It should be a gold mine for him."

With a light squeeze to her hand, he rested his cheek against hers. "I imagine we'll run into Evan and Daphne before the night is over. Right now I have something more important to talk to you about," he murmured close to her ear. "We're going to have to set a wedding date. Quickly."

The urgency in his voice caused her to ease her head back and latch her gaze to his. "Why? Has something happened?"

"I'm not sure. Mom told me today that Jameson and Van have started making wedding plans. To what extent, I can only guess. I can't ask. It would look too suspicious. But we can't let them beat us to the altar. Dad just might change his mind and say his eldest son has given the John family its first wedding and that might be enough to satisfy his demands."

Unease swept through her for many reasons. First of all, she needed the money Maddox was going to give her for playing along with his fake marriage. And secondly, crazy or not, she wasn't yet ready to give up this time she was spending with Maddox. With each passing day, he was growing more and more important to her. Stupid or not, she wanted to think that their time together was going to last for at least the year they'd bargained on.

"Maddox, what are we going to do? How are we going to suddenly get married? We've only been engaged for a few days. Our family and friends are just now getting used to the idea of the two of us together!"

"I know. I know. But you can see we're walking a tightrope, Adeline. We need to come up with some sort of reason for a quick wedding without sending up red flags. How long does it take to plan a big, fancy wedding, anyway?"

If the whole situation hadn't been so serious, she would have laughed at his question. Instead, she stifled a groan. "Some couples plan for a year or even two."

He shook his head. "Won't work. Our wedding will have to be planned at supersonic speed. So you need to start planning—and fast!"

The more he talked, the more annoyed she was becoming. "Maybe we should stop dancing so I can go start planning," she suggested in a sarcastic voice.

His eyes narrowed as he studied the stubborn expression on her face. "Look, Adeline, if you can't handle this, maybe we should end it all right now."

"It appears to me that you're the one having trouble handling things," she told him. "You might try being a bit more reasonable. A fast wedding? Okay. I'm all for it. The faster we do the deed, the quicker we can end this farce!"

She blasted the last remark at him just as the song came to an end and, deciding she needed some space to cool off, she said, "The music has stopped. You can let go of me."

"I have no intentions of letting you go. We're going to keep dancing."

What was it about this man that made her want to kiss him and in the next moment kick his shins?

"Why bother? By now most everyone in Bronco knows we're engaged."

"*Happily* engaged. That's the key word, Adeline—happy."

The music started again, and this time when they danced, he held her even more tightly.

"I'm bursting with happiness," she quipped. "I'm sure you can see it bubbling on my face."

He looked at her, then, shaking his head, he put a hand at the back of her head and drew her cheek next to his. Everything inside Adeline went soft and helpless.

"Forgive me, Adeline. I've sounded like a real jerk."

"Thank you for recognizing that," she told him. "And for what it's worth, I haven't exactly been a model of sweetness. I think we're both feeling too much pressure. The best thing we can do is plan this out rationally and calmly."

Only she couldn't remain calm while he was holding her so close. Nor could she think about anything except the way he was making her feel. The heat of his body was radiating right through her clothing while his hard thighs were brushing against hers.

"You're right, Adeline. We can't panic now. I'll come up with some reason for a quick wedding. In the meantime, you start thinking about a dress and cake and all that sort of thing."

From as early as her teenage years, she'd carried around an image of her dream wedding. She'd even told her parents exactly what she wanted when it came time for her to exchange vows with the man she loved. Back then, all those details had seemed so important to her. Now, she could hardly remember them. The only thing that mattered was that Maddox would be standing next to her. He would be the man slipping a wedding band onto her finger. None of this made sense.

"Adeline, are you okay? Are you still angry with me?"

Tomorrow she might regret her behavior, but tonight she didn't care.

Pressing the front of her body more tightly to his, she murmured close to his ear, "I'm not angry. I was only thinking how glad I'll be when we are finally married."

His nose nuzzled the side of her hair. "That's my girl."

During the next hour, the crowd grew until the dance floor was practically elbow to elbow. Maddox and Adeline decided it was a good time to grab some refreshments and find a place to sit while they waited for the area to clear.

"Looks like the refreshment tables are just as popular as the dance floor," Adeline said as she and Maddox walked hand in hand through the throngs of partygoers. "We're going to be lucky if we find an empty hay bale to sit on."

"I'm thinking—" He paused and gestured toward a group of people circled around a white-haired older lady sitting in a folding director's chair. She was dressed in a bright pink blouse and a deep purple skirt that billowed to the ground. A sparkly lavender scarf was tied around head. "Look, Adeline, there's Winona Cobbs. Do you know her?"

"Not personally, but I have heard of her. A former coworker of mine visited Winona's fortune-telling shop. She said Winona was so spot-on about her life that it made the hair on the back of her neck stand up. I recall her saying Winona is in her nineties. If that's true, she looks good for her age."

"Ninety-five, last I heard. Pretty spry to be out and about at an outdoor dance, don't you think?"

Adeline nodded. "I can only wish I make it to ninety-five, much less attend a dance."

Maddox tugged on her hand. "Come on. I see Evan and Daphne sitting next to her. Let's go say hello."

Once they reached the group and greeted the married couple, Evan introduced Maddox and Adeline to his great-grandmother, Winona.

"This couple just got engaged," Evan told the old woman. "I'm sure they'd appreciate your well-wishes."

Winona's keen eyes darted over Adeline, then moved to Maddox. After a thoughtful stretch of silence, she reached for Adeline's hand and gently patted the back of it. "Congratulations," she said. "You two will be happy if you focus on the important things."

As Winona spoke the words, she pierced Maddox with a look that left him feeling as if she could see every thought circling around in his head.

Uncomfortable with that idea, he looked away from Winona and over to Adeline. Her brown eyes were misty, and he realized this was the second time he'd seen her get emotional over their engagement. Could Wes be right, he wondered. Would this plan of his eventually hurt Adeline? Maddox could never allow her to be hurt. Nothing was worth putting her through any kind of pain. Not even the Double J.

That revelation prompted him to wrap an arm around Adeline's shoulders and pull her close to his side. "You shouldn't cry, sweetheart. Winona says we're going to be happy. And Winona should know."

Adeline smiled, then surprised him by leaning in and pressing a kiss on his cheek. "I'm fine. It's just that I get a little emotional when I think about the future. *Our* future."

"Well, when Maddox says Winona should know, she does," Evan said with an affectionate glance at the old woman. "And speaking of engagements, have you two heard my great-grandmother's news? She's just gotten engaged to Stanley Sanchez. Look at her ring. It's unique and beautiful—just like her."

Winona held her hand out to reveal a rather large round amethyst stone surrounded by smaller diamonds and set upon an intricately carved band of white gold.

Winona's eyes twinkled. "Stanley found it inside a teapot at an antique sale we went to. We both knew for certain the ring was destined to be worn on my finger."

"I'd call Stanley a lucky guy. He found two treasures. You and the ring," Maddox told her, then glanced around the group that had circled around Winona. "I don't see Mr. Sanchez. Didn't he come to the dance tonight?"

Winona regarded him with a crafty look. "He went to say hello to a friend. He'll be back in a few minutes."

Evan flashed his great-grandmother a fond grin. "Trust me, Stanley won't be away from Winona's side for long. She's his lady love."

Daphne was in the process of telling them just how much Stanley doted on his fiancée when a rail-thin middle-aged man rushed up to Winona.

"Ms. Cobbs, you're just the person I wanted to see. My friends and I have been having a debate about these Bobby Stone sightings. I think it's his ghost trying to haunt Bronco, but my friends are calling me a kook. We want to know what you think."

Adeline and Maddox exchanged questioning glances. Meanwhile Winona thoughtfully tapped a bony finger against her chin.

"I have heard about the sightings," Winona told him. "But I can't say much about them. I haven't received any signs about Bobby Stone. Perhaps if I could hold an item that belonged to him, I might receive some signals."

Signs? Sure, Maddox thought. Signs like those he and his brothers had received when they'd been kids, pretending the Double J was being invaded by Martians.

The man snapped his fingers. "There's someone here at the party who can get you something of Bobby's. Pleases don't leave, Ms. Cobbs. I'll be back with her in a few minutes."

Winona assured him that she'd stay put, and after the man rushed away, Maddox looked over at Evan.

"Does this type of thing happen often?"

Evan shrugged. "Grandmother sees all kinds of people and...things that others can't see. It's strange. But what can I say? I run a ghost tour business."

Maddox grinned. "Yeah. This mystical thing runs in the family."

Adeline put a hand on his arm. "Let's stay and see what happens. Winona might get some sort of communication. And I'm intrigued by this Bobby Stone thing."

"Sure. I wouldn't mind seeing this sign thing myself," Maddox told her. "I'll go get us something to drink while we wait."

He left the group and worked his way to the refreshment tables. By the time he returned to Adeline with two cups of apple cider, more people had gathered around Winona, including Stanley. The tall, robust man in his mid-eighties, dressed in a Western shirt and a black cowboy hat and boots, was standing directly beside his beloved's chair.

No faking for those two, Maddox thought ruefully as he spotted the older couple exchanging sweet glances.

Hell, what was he doing now? Feeling sorry for himself because Adeline wasn't looking at him with real love in her eyes? He needed someone to give him a swift kick in the ass.

Handing one of the cups of cider to Adeline, he said, "I thought you might like something warm."

"Thank you. This is nice."

He slipped his arm around her waist while thinking how much his life had changed since he'd met Adeline. Before, if someone had told him he'd be in the city park drinking cider and waiting to hear a ninety-five-year-old woman speak about a ghost, he would've pronounced them delusional. Beer and dance halls and a willing woman he forgot before the morning sun ever showed its face—that was Maddox John. Now he was pretending to be in love. Trying to make everyone believe he wanted to be a family man. It was laughable. Only he couldn't laugh.

Maddox's disturbing thoughts were suddenly interrupted as someone in the crowd announced in a loud voice, "Here she comes."

The group parted as a young woman with long, wavy blond hair hurried forward. From what Maddox could see, it looked as though she was carrying a small frame.

"Oh, I recognize her," Adeline said to Maddox in a hushed tone. "She's Sadie Chamberlin. She runs Sadie's Holiday House gift shop here in town."

"What does she have to do with the late Bobby Stone?" Maddox asked.

Adeline shook her head. "I don't have a clue."

Maddox looked over to Evan for an explanation. "Do you know?"

Evan nodded ruefully. "Bobby Stone was her brother-in-law. He was married to Sadie's late sister, Dana. She died in a car accident about a year ago."

Maddox said to Adeline, "This could end up being some kind of séance."

"Maddox, don't be crass," she scolded. "Sadie is such a nice person she makes shopping for gifts in Sadie's Holiday House even more fun. And I've seen for myself how hard she works to make the business go. I don't know anything about her private family life. But from a few comments I've heard her make, she didn't exactly have an easy childhood."

"Sounds like she doesn't need more uncertainty

in her life," Maddox said, then planted a kiss on her soft cheek. "And I'm not teasing about the seance, sweetheart. Winona might actually get some sort of vibes."

Surprised, Adeline looked at him. "You actually believe she has mystic powers?"

"I never put much stock in the idea before," Maddox told her. "But tonight when she looked at me, there was something in her eyes. I don't know... Let's just say I'm a bit of a believer."

He glanced over at Winona just as Sadie was handing her what he could now plainly see to be a framed photo.

"This was taken on their wedding day," Sadie told her. "Perhaps it can tell you something."

The old woman clutched the photo tightly and closed her eyes. In turn, the crowd around them grew eerily quiet.

"I'm feeling such sadness. And something is missing." Winona frowned as though her mind was struggling to break through a fog. "A vision is coming to me. It's a puzzle. But a piece is missing."

"I know what the missing piece is," a man in the crowd called out. "It's Dana. Bobby is missing his wife."

The suggestion put a pained look on Sadie's face. "I don't think that's the case," she said to Winona. "My sister's marriage to Bobby wasn't a happy one. They divorced about six months before he died. So I doubt he's missing her—even in another dimension."

Rumbles and grumbles rippled through the crowd, and some even began to walk away. Maddox supposed they were disappointed that Winona hadn't conjured up a real apparition.

Winona said, "Marriage is the greatest gift. But it's not to be taken lightly."

"Marriage ain't to be taken at all," an old man from the back of the gathering yelled.

The remark produced a spate of laughter from the folks who were still standing around. Clearly, the crowd had assumed Winona was talking about Bobby and Dana taking their marriage vows lightly. But Maddox didn't think so. Winona had been gazing directly at him when she'd spoken her sage words of wisdom.

Did the old woman actually know he was faking his way to the altar? Maddox was willing to believe she could *see* things, but he wasn't ready to accept the idea of her seeing *that* much.

Trying to shake away the weird premonition, he turned to Adeline. "Let's go see if the dance floor has cleared. My boots are itching to make another round."

She smiled at him. "If that's the case, then we'd better go take care of your itchy boots."

They began walking in the direction of the dance floor, and as they worked their way through the milling crowd, Maddox grew achingly aware of her leg brushing against his, the subtle scent of flowers drifting from her long hair.

Oh yes, he had an itch—however, it was far from his boots. But Maddox wasn't going to admit such a thing to her. One of the main stipulations she'd made in their deal was no sex. But what if she changed her mind? Did he want her to change her mind?

"You must know lots of people, Maddox," she commented. "I've noticed several looking at you."

Her voice broke through his erotic thoughts, and he gave her the most innocent smile he could muster. "They're not looking at me, Adeline. Their attention is all on you. And by the way, have I told you how lovely you look tonight? I like your dress. It makes you look sweet."

Laughing softly, she squeezed his arm. "Maddox, you've missed your calling being a rancher. You're getting so good at this acting thing, you ought to consider going to Hollywood. You know, Western movies are making a comeback of sorts. You'd make a perfect gunslinger."

Normally that kind of remark would have him playfully feigning a hurt look. But he was suddenly struck with the realization that he didn't have to feign disappointment. Her skeptical attitude toward him did actually sting.

"Gunslinger, eh? Well, at least you wouldn't cast me as the coward hiding behind the bar."

The smile she gave him caused dimples to bracket her cheeks, and it was all Maddox could do to keep from pulling her into his arms and ravishing her face with kisses.

"You hiding behind a bar? Oh no. I'll always re-member that first night I saw you sitting at the bar in DJ's Deluxe. You looked like you'd just ridden in from the range and were spoiling for a fight."

His lips twisted to a wry slant. "You didn't want any part of me."

Her lashes lowered as she passed a probing glance over his face. "You told Rusty that I was going to be your wife."

His fingertips gently touched her cheek. "That was just wishful thinking, sweetheart."

Her lips parted, and the next thing he expected to hear was another mocking laugh. But she didn't laugh. She quickly looked away from him and said, "Come on. The band is playing one of my favorite songs. And we need to get those itchy boots of yours taken care of."

And the other itch he'd developed would have to be cured with a series of long, cold showers. But to win a big share of the Double J, he could endure anything—even a year without sex, Maddox thought ruefully. Besides, he could always make up for the sacrifice after he and Adeline divorced.

It's not to be taken lightly.

As they were about to step onto the dance floor, Winona's words slipped through his mind, and he paused to look at Adeline.

"Do you believe Winona can see things?" he asked.

"If you're asking me if she's a true psychic, I'm

not even sure that kind of person actually exists. But I do think Winona understands people, and she uses her years of wisdom to explain certain happenings." Tilting her head to one side, she gave him an impish smile. "Why, Maddox, I think the old woman got to you—maybe just a little."

Yeah, weird or not, Winona or something had gotten to him tonight.

Forcing a chuckle, he led her onto the dance floor and into the circle of his arms.

"Halloween is coming. It's the season for getting spooked," he said.

Her brown eyes twinkled as she looked up at him. "Scared?"

There were plenty of things going on in his life that should be scaring him, but Adeline had pegged him correctly. He wasn't a man to back down or run from a fight.

Pressing his cheek against the side of her hair, he murmured near her ear. "Not with you in my arms, sweetheart."

Chapter Ten

Two days later, Adeline was standing on the sidewalk, staring into the display window of Ever After, the one and only bridal boutique in Bronco, when a female voice called out to her.

"Adeline! How wonderful to run into you like this!"

Glancing down the sidewalk, Adeline was momentarily caught off guard to see Mimi John striding rapidly toward her.

Quickly gathering herself, she greeted Maddox's mother. "Hello, Mimi. It's good to see you."

Mimi gave her a tight hug and a kiss on the cheek. "Oh my, you're looking more beautiful every day. It's no wonder Maddox can't quit talking about you."

Adeline didn't quite believe Mimi's observation, but on the other hand, Maddox was definitely a guy who liked to spread it on. She stepped back. "Are you out shopping today?"

Mimi gestured behind her to the entrance of Beaumont and Rossi's Fine Jewels, Bronco's premier jewelry store, where Maddox had purchased her fantastic engagement ring.

"I've ordered something special for Randall's birthday—a monogrammed money clip. It doesn't match up to the gold-and-silver belt buckle I got for him last year, but what do you get a man who has everything?" she asked with a little laugh.

"I understand," Adeline told her. "My mother has the same problem with Dad."

Mimi's smile turned clever as she turned her attention to the boutique's display window. "Looks like you're getting wedding ideas."

Oh Lord, this was awkward, Adeline thought. True, Maddox wanted to speed up their engagement, but sharing anything with Mimi at this point might not be compatible with Maddox's plans.

"Well, since Maddox has slipped a ring on my finger, I can't help but dream about wedding dresses. I was just looking at this one in the window," she told her, which was true enough. "It's beautiful. But I'm not all that fond of the mermaid style."

"Why don't we go in and have a look around?" Mimi suggested. "I'd love to hear your ideas of the kind of dress you want. And trust me, I won't tell

Maddox a thing. After all, a groom isn't supposed to know how his bride is going to look on the big day."

Not seeing any polite way to refuse, Adeline gave her a warm smile. "I'd love for us to look together."

Bells chimed as they entered the shop, and Adeline's first impressions were the faint scent of roses and a wide swath of dark parquet flooring that stretched between compartments of hanging dresses. The entire area was illuminated with soft lighting that reminded Adeline of moon glow on a summer night. Vases of fresh flowers sat on antique tables, while wing-backed chairs covered in pale rose brocade provided customer seating.

"I've never been in here," Adeline admitted as she glanced around her. "I always thought whenever I planned to get married, I'd go to Billings or some other city to a big bridal store. But this is lovely."

Mimi said, "I'm glad you think so. And I'm sure when the time comes, you'll find the perfect dress right here at Ever After. I know the owner, Patrice Gibbons. Given ample time, she's always glad to do a special order for a customer."

Ample time. Adeline only wished she knew how much time she had before Maddox was going to announce a wedding date. Yesterday when she'd spoken to him on the phone, he'd told her he was still trying to come up with a feasible reason for them to marry quickly.

"Well, I'm not sure I'd want to order a dress," she told Mimi, then as she saw the woman's brows arch in question, she quickly added, "I mean, it might need to be altered and all that sort of thing. I think I'd really rather just find something off the rack."

Mimi was about to reply when a woman who appeared to be in her mid-thirties, with dark auburn hair twisted into a chignon, walked up to them.

"Hello, Mrs. John, it's nice to see you. Are you here to find a mother-of-the-groom gown for Jameson and Vanessa's wedding?"

Mimi glanced at Adeline, then back to the boutique owner. "No. Unfortunately, they haven't finalized their wedding plans yet." With a hand on Adeline's arm, she drew her forward. "Patrice, I want you to meet Adeline Longsworth. She and Maddox are engaged, and she's dreaming about wedding dresses. Do you mind if we take a peek at a few?"

"Oh, so that slippery son of yours has finally found his soul mate," Patrice said to Mimi, then turned to Adeline with an outstretched hand. "Congratulations, Ms. Longsworth. It's a pleasure to meet you. Please look all you like. If you find something you'd like to try on, I'll be happy to help you. And just so you know, I have an expert seamstress who deals with any and all alterations you might need to make the fit perfect."

The chimes over the door sounded as another customer entered the boutique, and Patrice left them to search through the numerous dresses that were grouped according to hem length.

While Adeline studied a tea-length dress with a

tulle skirt, Mimi looked over to the entrance of the boutique where Patrice was welcoming other customers.

"Oh, a pair of celebrities have come to shop at Ever After," she said. "That's two of the Hawkins sisters. I recognize them from the Bronco Heights Summer Rodeo. Did you see them perform? They were great."

Adeline glanced around to see Audrey Hawkins and her older sister, Brynn walking into the lobby area. Both women were very attractive with Brynn being tall and willowy with a lovely brown complexion and long dark brown hair that curled on her shoulders, while Audrey was petite with a golden brown complexion and long black wavy hair.

"Yes, I did see them roping and riding at the rodeo," Adeline told her. "I also had the good fortune to meet them one night in DJs Deluxe. Since then I've bumped into them around town a few times. If they come our way, I'll introduce you."

"I'd love that," Mimi told her.

Adeline barely had time to make the suggestion when the two rodeo stars headed their way.

"Hi Adeline! Is that you?" Audrey, the younger of the two asked.

Adeline gave both women a warm smile. "Yes, it's me. Nice to see you both again."

"Are you looking for a bridal gown for yourself?" Brynn asked.

The question had her darting a glance at Mimi. Maddox's mother was smiling with pride.

"Well, I'm looking and dreaming. You see I've just recently become engaged to Maddox John. So we've not set any kind of date yet." She gestured to Mimi who was standing at her side. "I'd like to introduce my fiance's mother, Mimi John. And Mimi, this is Audrey and Brynn Hawkins. You know them as fabulous rodeo riders."

"I certainly do," Mimi agreed.

The three women exchanged greetings and then Mimi asked, "So which one of you beautiful ladies is looking for a wedding gown?"

Brynn motioned to Audrey. "My little sister is the one who's getting married—to Jack Burris. His brother is Geoff, the famous rodeo cowboy. I'm sure you ladies have heard of him and his family."

"Yes we've attended a couple of the competitions here in Bronco," Adeline told her, then smiled at Audrey. "Congratulations. Have you set a date?"

"Thank you," she said, then shook her head. "No. We haven't decided on a date yet. With both of us working the rodeo circuit, the date will have to be between seasons."

"And don't forget. You two will have to work around the promotional event for the upcoming Mistletoe Rodeo."

Audrey playfully rolled her eyes and gestured to Brynn. "She always has to be the big sister and remind me of our schedules. But she's right. We have to plan ahead. And we're really looking forward to competing in the Mistletoe Rodeo along with the Burris brothers."

"We'll certainly be attending," Mimi said.

"I wouldn't miss it, either," Adeline assured both women.

The sisters talked for a few more minutes before they moved away and turned their attention to the dresses.

Once the women were out of earshot, Mimi said, "Adeline, I hope you won't think I'm being a nosy mother-in-law-to-be, but I noticed you told the Hawkins sisters you hadn't set a wedding date. So when are you and Maddox planning to wed?"

Adeline tried to keep the frozen look off her face as she glanced at Mimi. "Of course I don't think you're being nosy, Mimi. Maddox is your son. Naturally, you're curious. But right now I'm not exactly sure what he's thinking."

Mimi's smile was gentle. "What are *you* thinking? Your feelings are just as important as his."

Too bad her marriage was only going to last for a year, Adeline thought. Mimi was going to be a caring and understanding mother-in-law.

"Well, I'm—uh—so in love with Maddox, I'd be happy to marry him tomorrow," she said as a blush stung her cheeks. "But that isn't possible. And I don't want him to feel rushed."

Smiling gently, Mimi patted the top of her hand. "Don't worry. I won't let on to Maddox that you were looking at wedding dresses today."

At this moment, Adeline refused to let herself feel like a heel. Even if her and Maddox's marriage would be a little unorthodox, bonding with his mother like this was important to Adeline.

For the next forty minutes, the two women browsed through the display of exquisite bridal gowns, and then Adeline suggested they go for coffee at Bronco Java and Juice. Mimi was thrilled with the idea, and the two ended up spending another hour together over coffee.

Once they finally said their goodbyes, Adeline walked to her car and immediately pulled out her cell phone.

Maddox answered on the third ring. "Hi, babe! What's up?"

Babe, sweetheart, sweetie. He'd gotten into the habit of calling her all sorts of endearments, and though she figured she should call him out on it and remind him of their *fake* situation, she didn't. Mainly because she adored the sound of his voice calling her those loving names.

"Am I interrupting anything? Do you have a minute to talk?"

"I have more than a minute. We just got back from doctoring a few cows. I'm headed to the house for coffee."

She groaned, then followed the sound with a soft laugh. "That's what I just had with your mother."

"My mother! I don't see your car parked here in the ranch yard. Where are you?"

"In town. I ran into Mimi on the sidewalk. She'd been shopping, and she saw me standing in front of Ever After. I couldn't avoid her!"

"What is Ever After?" he asked. "Some naughty place you shouldn't have been visiting? Like a fantasy shop?"

She groaned again. "Oh, Maddox, I truly wonder about your mind sometimes! Ever After is a bridal boutique. A store where you buy wedding dresses."

"Oh. So Mom thinks you have wedding dresses on your mind? Honey, that's great!"

Adeline massaged her forehead with her fingertips. "You think so? I've been kind of worried. She asked me straight out about our wedding plans—about setting a date—and I had to dance around the issue. I told her I was so in love with you that I honestly would marry you tomorrow."

There was a long pause, and then he said in a low voice, "You did, did you?"

"Well, yes. And believe me, she ate it up."

After another stretch of silence, he replied, "I see. So that was all for effect."

"Of course. What other reason would I have for saying such a thing?"

"None," he said. "None at all."

She frowned. "Maddox, you're not sounding like yourself. What's wrong? You think I've messed up and your mother is going to suspect something?"

"No! Nothing is wrong." He cleared his throat,

then said, "Actually, I'm pleased that you two got on so well."

"We did, actually. We had a nice time together."

"I'm glad. Because I—I think I've come up with a solution to our need for a hasty marriage."

She sat straight up in the car seat. "Tell me."

"I'm going to tell Mom that you're pregnant."

The people passing by on the sidewalk in front of her car went unnoticed as she struggled to digest his words. Finally, she gasped out, "Pregnant! Maddox John, that is…diabolical! It's…indecent!"

"Maybe so. But it'll work," he said firmly.

"For how long?" she practically shouted the question at him. "In a couple of months, your parents, my parents and everyone else is going to want to know why my belly isn't growing! You know, women don't exactly stay the same when they're pregnant!"

"Calm down, Adeline. Do you think I'm stupid or something? I see pregnant cows and horses every day. I know their bellies get big."

She squeezed her eyes shut as she tried to hold on to her temper. "So now you're comparing me to a cow or a horse. Maddox, I—"

"Listen, I'm a cowboy, a rancher," he interrupted. "Maybe I'm not using the best terms, and I'm sorry about that. But I do understand what you're trying to say. We'll worry about how to deal with that later. After two or three months, we'll say something happened—that you had a miscarriage. Those tragedies do happen."

Unconvinced, she said in a sarcastic voice, "In cows, too, I suppose."

"No. That's pretty rare. But you're not a cow."

"So sweet of you to notice. Right now I'd give anything to be a cow," she said through clenched teeth. "I'd kick you so hard you'd land in the next county!"

"Aw, Adeline. You're worrying too much. Just stay focused on the end results—the money you're going to get. You'll be free of your father's interference. You'll be able to start the travel business you've had your heart set on."

Thank goodness there were miles between them and he couldn't see the tears brimming in her eyes. She never wanted him to guess how her heart had changed its wants and wishes. Somewhere along the way, she'd forgotten all about building a travel agency of her own. Her heart was set on him and being his wife.

She stifled a helpless sigh. "Okay, Maddox. If you think this idea of yours will work, then I'll do my best to go along. I'll give my parents the news in the morning. But I hope you're right about this. Otherwise, we're going to look like lowdown scammers."

"This is going to work, sweetheart. You start picking out a wedding dress for real, 'cause you're going to be wearing it soon."

Diabolical. Indecent.

Later that night, Maddox tossed from one side of the bed to the other as Adeline's words refused to leave him alone. She believed he was ruthless and conniving. And perhaps he was. But he didn't want to put himself in such a sorry league. And he especially didn't like her labeling him as a scammer. She needed to understand he was backed in a corner. Announcing that Adeline was pregnant was the only solution he could come up with to speed up this process of getting the two of them married.

The next morning, he climbed out of bed earlier than usual and made his way to the kitchen. Fortunately, he found his mother alone, preparing the family breakfast.

"Good morning, Maddox. You're up early. Have something special to do today?"

"Morning, Mom." He walked over to where she was kneading biscuit dough on a large cutting board. After dropping a kiss on her cheek, he said, "And yes, I do have something special to do. Talk to you."

She darted him a clever glance as she pushed a metal cutter into the soft dough. "I think I already know what you're going to say. You and Adeline want to get married sooner rather than later."

Adeline must've made quite an impression on his mother yesterday, Maddox thought. "How did you guess?"

She began arranging the biscuits into a large cast iron skillet. "Well, let's just say when I look at you two together, I see the sparks."

"I—uh—I'm glad you've noticed, Mom, because—" He drew in a deep breath and blew it out. When he'd first been struck with this idea, he'd thought it would be easy. But now that he was actually facing his mother, the words were jammed in his throat. "Adeline is pregnant."

A stunned look came over her face while her floured hands dropped to her sides. "Pregnant! Oh my. Are you sure?"

He nodded, then coughed to cover his embarrassment. "Yes. She only found out yesterday. One of those quick test things. You're probably familiar with those."

Mimi's face brightened with sudden dawning. "Oh, so that's why she—"

"She what?"

Smiling faintly, she shook her head. "Nothing, son. I'm only wondering how you feel about this. Plenty of times I've heard you say you had no desire to be a daddy. Now that's going to change. I hope you're not disappointed."

Not wanting his mother to read the emotions that were no doubt traipsing across his face, he walked to the opposite end of the cabinet and poured himself a cup of coffee.

He said, "I admit, I used to swear I never wanted kids. But that was before I met Adeline. She's changed me. Now that I have her in my life, I'm feeling different about everything. So to answer your question, I'm pretty thrilled about this coming baby. The timing might have been better, and we didn't exactly plan on this. But we love each other so much we got a little careless."

His mother wiped her hands, then walked over and gave him a tight hug. "You don't have to explain, son. Your father and I were young once and madly in love. I understand. And he will, too."

"You think so?" His gaze dropped to the toes of his boots. "I'm not sure. That's why I wanted to give you the news first."

She clicked her tongue in a reproving way. "Maddox, you're a grown man, not a teenager. This is your and Adeline's private business. But now that this has happened, I certainly understand why you want to speed up your wedding plans."

Finally, the crux of the matter was out, sending a flood of relief rushing through him. "The sooner the better. And I'm wondering if you'd be willing to help Adeline get things organized? She's all gung ho for a huge, fancy wedding—just the kind you and Dad want for our family. And I don't want her to miss out just because the baby is limiting our time."

The wide smile on her face should have made Maddox feel ashamed of his deceit. But it didn't. For now he had made his mother happy. Wasn't that enough justification?

Hugging him again, she said, "It will be a joy, Maddox. On top of a wedding to end all weddings, you're going to give your parents a grandchild. It's all wonderful."

Resisting the urge to cross his fingers behind his back, he said, "I hope everyone else feels like you do, Mom."

* * *

Later that same morning on the Lazy L, Adeline gave her parents the news about her pregnancy, and their reaction had been everything she'd expected—her mother had burst into tears and her father had been so furious he'd slammed out of the house.

Hours had passed since then, and Louis still hadn't returned. Naomi was pacing around the kitchen while Adeline made an effort to eat a grilled cheese sandwich for lunch. Which was quite a struggle, considering she had to swallow each bite past the huge lump lodged in her throat.

"You're picking at your food, Adeline." Naomi paused in front of the table and eyed the partially eaten sandwich on her daughter's plate. "Is it morning sickness?"

The urge to laugh and cry hit Adeline at the same time, but she managed to block the strangled sound before it passed her lips. "No. I'm just not hungry."

Naomi regarded her with narrowed eyes. "You need to talk to the doctor about your appetite. The baby needs nutrition. I take it you've already seen a doctor?"

Oh Lord, here we go, Adeline thought. "Not yet. I just took an at-home pregnancy test yesterday. I haven't had time to make an appointment."

Naomi's reaction was to sigh and press a hand to her forehead. "I realize these things happen when two people are in love. But you're a smart girl. I thought you'd be more cautious."

"Passion and smartness usually don't go together." If they did, she wouldn't be experiencing such tender feelings about Maddox, Adeline thought. She'd have the willpower to tell him to keep his money and she'd walk away from the whole farce. Instead, her mind was stuck on the way it felt when he held her in his arms and kissed her.

"Well, I have to look on the bright side," Naomi said in a resigned voice. "You're going to give me a grandchild. And I'm thrilled about that—even though the news has crushed Louis."

"I hate to tell you this, Mom, but you hardly looked thrilled."

Naomi walked around to Adeline's chair and rested her hands on her shoulders.

"I'm sorry, Adeline. I'm not worrying about you. I'm sure Maddox is going to take extra loving care of you. It's your father that's putting this strained look on my face. I'm wondering how we're going to get through any of the coming days with him being so stiff-necked. It's not going to be easy. Not for me, at least." She dabbed at the moisture collecting in her eyes. "A wedding, a coming baby—this is a special time in your life. I want to be a part of it."

Adeline patted her mother's hand. "You will be, Mom. Don't worry. Dad will—"

The rest of Adeline's words remained unspoken as the outside door to the kitchen suddenly opened. Cold wind whipped past Louis as he stepped inside the room and hung his cowboy hat on a hall tree.

Adeline and her mother exchanged uncertain glances as he walked over to the table.

His expression grim, his gaze passed back and forth between his wife and daughter. "What are you two doing? Discussing what a bastard I am?"

"Louis, please. We—" Naomi stopped abruptly when Louis raised his hand.

"You don't have to say anything, Naomi. I know what I am." He raked a hand through his graying hair, then, moving over to the table, he curved both hands over the back of a chair as though he needed to brace himself. "I've been out riding on the west range and doing some hard thinking."

"Dad, I know you're disappointed in me—"

He interrupted her with a shake of his head. "No. I'm disappointed in myself. I need to admit the fact that I've been a terrible father. And probably an even worse husband. I didn't start out that way." He looked at his wife's strained face. "I was a different man when we were young and first married. You remember?"

Naomi nodded stiffly, and Adeline could see she was caught somewhere between shock and fear.

"Yes," Naomi admitted quietly. "You had a tender side then."

The frown on his face turned to a look of agony. "Somehow, while I was trying to make a fortune and keep my family protected, I lost that part of me."

For the first time in Adeline's life, she saw remorse on her father's face, and the sight of it struck her deep. No matter how hard she'd tried to convince herself that his lack of love or admiration was of little consequence to her, she'd always needed him. Always prayed he would change.

"Dad, you don't have to say any of this. We've never expected you to be perfect."

He grunted. "No. But I expected it out of you, your mother and your sister. That was wrong of me, too."

Adeline was aware of her mother's hands tightening on her shoulders.

"Our daughter needs you now, Louis. And so do I," Naomi told him.

He nodded glumly. "I'll admit I've held a grudge against the Johns. And I never would've chosen one of Randall's sons to be my son-in-law or the father of my first grandchild. But, Adeline, I want you to be happy. And if this man is what you want, then I'm not going to stand in your way. We'll pay for our share of the wedding and help you in whatever way you might need."

Staggered by her father's sudden about-face, she stared at him.

Did this mean he might agree to give her the funds to start her own travel agency, too? No. She wasn't going to mention that issue. For now her parents were expecting her to be focused on her husband and baby. Not a career. And oddly enough, she'd made a pact with Maddox and she fully intended to honor the deal.

"Dad, are you serious?" she finally asked.

"I can't explain myself, Adeline. But take my word for it. I'm serious."

With a little cry of joy, she jumped up and rushed around the table to where he was standing.

Hugging him tightly, she pressed her cheek against his chest, and for the first time in a long time, she felt as if she truly had a father. "Oh, Dad. I love you. You've made me happier than you could know."

Louis gently patted her back, and as Adeline looked over at her mother's wobbly smile, she realized that no matter what happened with her marriage, her father's change of heart was a monumental breakthrough.

Maddox hadn't expected his father to be thrilled about Adeline's pregnancy news. In fact, he'd thought Randall would probably chastise his son for his reckless behavior. Instead, he'd been over the moon at the idea of becoming a grandfather. Not only that, he'd insisted he was going to open his wallet as wide as necessary for their wedding to be the most beautiful and massive ceremony the folks around Bronco had ever witnessed.

Maddox supposed the biggest surprise, however, was how Louis and Naomi Longsworth had welcomed him into their home. There had been no recriminations or threats thrown at him. When he'd gone to the Lazy L to meet them, they had greeted him warmly. The couple had also opened their stacked banking account to help with the cost of the wedding and had even been over to the Double J on several occasions to help his parents deal with many of the preparations.

What a difference a baby made, Maddox thought as he walked through the enormous barn where the wedding ceremony would be held tomorrow. His mother's reaction hadn't been that much of a surprise to Maddox. She loved all her children equally and a grandchild from any one of them would make her happy. It was his father's response that had caught him off guard. Maddox couldn't remember a time he'd made his father this happy or put such a look of pride on his face. Any praise Randall dished out to his children was usually directed at Jameson, who never seemed to disappoint their father.

Now Randall was eying Maddox with genuine approval and though a part of him was basking in the light of his father's admiration, the other part of him was weighted with guilt. He hated deceiving his parents in such a way. He also hated to think of how devastated they were going to be when they learned there would be no baby. But his and Adeline's plans were already in motion. He couldn't let his guilty conscience ruin them now.

But not everyone had been slapping his back and shaking his hand over the news of his upcoming wedding and expectant baby. No, his brother Jameson was still calling him all kinds of a jerk for carrying his coldhearted scheme to such a degree. He'd even gone so far as to refuse to act as Maddox's best man. As a result, Maddox had asked Dawson to do the deed and, thankfully, his younger brother had been happy to oblige.

"Who would have ever thought this old barn could look like this? Isn't it dreamy, Maddox?"

Maddox glanced behind him to see his sister, Charity, gazing up at the high-beamed ceiling draped with strips of delicate white chiffon and endless strings of small, clear lights. A romantic at heart, she'd been enjoying every moment of the wedding planning and had helped tirelessly with decorations, invitations and had even taken charge of the dresses for Adeline's six bridesmaids.

He shook his head in amazement. For the past two weeks, dozens of workers had been going around the clock to transform the barn into a fairy-tale setting. Even now, more than a dozen employees with the catering service were busy out in the adjoining white tent, finishing the last details of the dining tables, the bar where countless bottles of champagne and spirits would be served, and the tables displaying the ice sculptures Louis Longsworth had special ordered for the occasion.

"I'll say this. It doesn't look like the same barn that normally houses our haying equipment," Maddox said. "And this renovation has all been accomplished in a matter of days. Just laying down this portable flooring was a major undertaking. It's all amazing to me."

"There were probably twenty men working on the

floor at one time. And it turned out so gorgeous," Charity replied.

"Yeah, everyone has been working so hard to get everything ready. And I'm sure some people are wondering why we didn't have the wedding at The Association or a church in town. But this ranch is my home and home is where the heart is. Being married here on the Double J and in high style is going to make me very happy," Maddox told her.

"You made the perfect choice, Maddox." Stepping up to his side, Charity wrapped her arm through his. "When they remove the chairs after the ceremony, it will be perfect for dancing. Are you getting nervous about the first dance?"

Only last night, as they'd gone through rehearsal, Maddox had playfully waltzed Adeline over the floor. She'd laughed breathlessly, and he was hoping that tomorrow after the actual ceremony, she would be equally happy.

Since they'd announced her "pregnancy" two weeks ago, her moods had swung from joyous to glum and everything in between. He understood she was bothered about the deceit they were using on everyone. But there wasn't much he could do to change the facts of the situation.

He said, "The dance I can manage. I'm more concerned about getting my tongue tangled when the minister tells me to repeat the vows."

Charity laughed. "Tangled feet. Tangled tongue.

In the end it won't matter, dear brother. It's going to be a happy day for all of us," she said, then added in a sober tone, "except for Jameson. I just don't get him, Maddox. The two of you have always been so close. But he acts like he could care less that you're getting married. I think it's shameful. I even told him so."

"Hmm. And what did he tell you?"

She smirked. "To mind my own business. If you ask me, he's being a jerk."

Maddox shook his head. "Don't be hard on Jameson. He has plenty of other things on his mind. Like his own wedding." *And losing his majority share of the Double J,* Maddox thought. But that was hardly Maddox's fault. Jameson had his chance to make their parents' wishes come true, but he'd refused. Now Jameson resented Maddox for taking advantage of the situation. He didn't want his relationship with Jameson to be strained. But considering the circumstances, how could he go about fixing it?

"Pooh. Jameson and Vanessa are going to have a simple wedding. Hardly no planning at all," Charity said with a dismissive wave of her hand. "So where's Adeline? I thought she'd be here to see how the last of the decorations were coming together. I know she's going to swoon over the flowers. They look fabulous."

Since Maddox had first announced Adeline's fake pregnancy, their lives had turned into a wild whirlwind. Both of them had been so caught up in getting ready for the wedding, they'd hardly had a chance to spend much time together. Maddox had come to recognize he missed her company and the fun they'd had together while the two of them had simply been dating.

"Adeline had to go into town for last-minute alterations on her dress. We'd planned on having supper together. But now I won't get to see her until we meet at the altar tomorrow."

Charity gave him a knowing smile. "I never thought I'd see you looking so in love. What made you think she was the one?"

Maddox chuckled. "What is this? A test?"

The smile on her pretty face turned sly. "Sort of. I'm curious. You know I've been dating Nick for a while now, and to be honest, I'm not hearing bells ring or birds sing or feeling any sort of zing when he reaches for my hand. Should I?"

Did he honestly look like he was in love? Had this acting thing gone on for so long it had actually caused him to morph into the character of a man in love? Or was all the zinging he felt whenever he touched Adeline the real thing?

Forcing out a little laugh, he gave her shoulders a one-armed hug. "Trust me, sis, when you fall in love, you'll know it."

"Something borrowed, blue, old and new," Emily Longsworth repeated in a dreamy voice as she stood next to her sister and stared at the beautiful image Adeline made in the dresser mirror.

The dress Adeline had found at the Ever After bridal boutique was everything she'd ever dreamed of wearing on her wedding day. The white silk, overlaid with delicate floral lace, had a formfitting bodice with a sweetheart neckline and a deep V in the back, where it fastened together with a row of tiny pearl buttons. The long sleeves were tight and ended in a point on the top of her hands, while the slightly flared skirt fell in gentle folds to the floor, where it covered a pair of white, crystal-embellished high heels.

"I have the something borrowed if you're willing to wear it," Emily went on. "My pearl hair clasp. The one Mom gave me for my twentieth birthday. It'll match the tiny pearls on your veil."

Adeline smiled at her younger sister. Emily had been thrilled when Adeline had asked her to be her maid of honor, but her greatest joy had been the news that her big sister was expecting a baby. Since she'd arrived home from college three days ago, Emily had done little more than talk about becoming an aunt and babysitting the tyke after he or she arrived.

Each time Adeline looked at her sister's beaming face, she felt a bit sick inside. And it wasn't only her sister that she was deceiving. The announcement that she was carrying Maddox's child had put happy faces on the Johns and the Longsworths also. No matter how awful and confused she felt about the situation, Adeline wanted both families to remain happy. Especially on this, her wedding day.

"I'd be honored to wear it, sissy. Will you put in my hair for me?"

While Emily was attaching the pearl clasp to Adeline's upswept dark hair, Mimi approached her with a ring. The piece of jewelry consisted of a single blue sapphire in an antique setting.

"Naomi and I thought this would work perfectly for your something old and blue. The ring was handed down to Randall through his grandmother. It's been in the John family years before her."

Adeline was humbled that Maddox's parents wanted her to wear a family heirloom. "Oh, it's lovely, Mimi. Just perfect. Thank you for allowing me to wear it."

Mimi slipped it on Adeline's finger, then gently kissed her cheek. "You look incredibly beautiful, my dear. You're going to take everyone's breath away. Especially Maddox's."

Her heart panged with regret, but she did her best to give her future mother-in-law a smile. "I hope you're right, Mimi."

"Now that you have something borrowed and blue, you need something new," Naomi said from across the room.

Adeline looked around just as her mother joined her and the other two women gathered around the dressing mirror. A flat black velvet box was in her hands.

"Your father and I bought this for your wedding day. We hope you'll wear it as your something new."

She flipped open the lid for Adeline to see, and all the women gasped. Especially Adeline. The diamond-clustered necklace and earrings lying on the black velvet glittered in the sunlight streaming through the bedroom window on the Double J.

"Oh! I don't know what to say." Struggling to hold back tears, she looked up at her mother. "For a long time, I was afraid Dad wouldn't even be at my wedding. Now my heart is full—that's all I can say."

"Let me have the honor," Emily said as she carefully plucked the piece of jewelry from its velvet nest and draped it around Adeline's neck. "And remember, Mom, I want something similar from you and Dad whenever I get married."

The women all laughed, including Adeline, but deep down she made a wish that when her sister did eventually get married, it would be to a man who truly loved her. Instead of merely pretending.

Hundreds of wedding guests filled the endless rows of chairs inside the cavernous barn. Trailing green vines intertwined with roses in colors ranging from pale yellow to deep burgundy adorned the large support beams running from the floor to the ceiling. Centered in front of the altar, a latticed archway was covered with the same flowers, while tall candle stands stood at intervals along both sides of the room. A white aisle runner, delicately embossed with entwined hearts, had been rolled out over the dark parquet flooring. Several feet behind and to the

left of the altar, a grand piano was spilling out clas-
sic tunes of love, while the very air inside the transformed barn was filled with the faint scent of roses.

As Maddox stood in a black tuxedo with Dawson to his immediate right, followed by a line of
five groomsmen, all dressed in matching tuxes, everything felt surreal. Was this really him about to
say a temporary goodbye to his freedom as a single
man? Had he and Adeline really fooled everyone in
the building? Or were they just fooling themselves?
And why did it hurt to look at Jameson and see the
shadow of disappointment in his eyes?

As Emily took her place as the maid of honor and
the young flower girl strewed fragrant rose petals
along the aisle, the questions circled in Maddox's
head like a merry-go-round. Until, finally, the pia-
nist struck up the bridal march and the guests rose.
Then Maddox turned his head just enough to look
down the aisle. The instant he spotted Adeline on her
father's arm, something in the middle of his chest
suddenly shattered like a piece of fragile glass. Frag-
ments of joy and pain and sheer disbelief showered
through him, leaving him stunned and trembling.

He'd never seen a more beautiful woman in his
life, and she was going to be his. Truly his.

*In name only, Maddox. Don't forget the pact you
made.*

Damn the pact. Damn everything, he mentally
cursed at the voice in his head. None of that mat-

tered anymore. The only thing that mattered was the woman who was about to become his wife.

Songs were sung by a male vocalist; candles were lit and prayers were spoken. Throughout the ceremony Adeline had to keep reminding herself that she wasn't actually taking part in a fairy tale. But the moment the minister pronounced them man and wife and Maddox placed his lips on hers, she realized she wasn't dreaming. And he definitely wasn't holding back on the kiss.

"Ladies and gentlemen, I present to you Mr. and Mrs. Maddox John."

The minister's introduction brought a round of applause from the guests, and then Maddox was hurrying her down the aisle toward the wide-open doorway of the barn.

She sensed a group of guests rushing behind them, and as soon as they stepped out into the late-afternoon sunshine, she was gathered up in an endless round of hugs and kisses.

The congratulations seemed to go on forever until Randall finally began encouraging everyone to head over to the reception area, which was located in a huge white tent erected directly next to the barn. Linen-dressed tables, each decorated with vases of fresh-cut flowers, tall candles and set with delicate china and intricately carved silverware, were set up beneath billows of white chiffon and trailing vines. Seating was provided by high-backed chairs covered with white lace, while ice sculptures in the shape of entwined hearts, lovebirds and a pair of cherubs were displayed on tables in the center of the dining area.

Even though Adeline had helped with the planning, she wasn't prepared for the sheer lavishness of the whole scene, and as she and Maddox made their way to the sweetheart table designated for the newlyweds, she looked at him in amazement.

"Our parents have both spent a fortune for this," she whispered close to his ear. "I feel like a phony."

He kissed her cheek, then whispered back, "Trust me, Adeline. This is exactly what our parents wanted. This is all their show. It's not for us. So let them enjoy showing off their children. And their wealth."

"I suppose you're right."

His grin was pure sexiness. "I'm always right. Now that I'm your husband, you're going to find that out."

She chuckled, and the hold he had on her waist tightened. The subtle touch caused her mind to leap ahead to their honeymoon, and she suddenly wondered how she was going to handle sleeping in the same room with him.

Chapter Eleven

The reception went on for hours and hours, or so it seemed to Maddox. The food, the cocktails, the many toasts and the endless rounds of well-wishers stopping by their table began to blur in his mind.

He was relieved when they finally moved back into the barn, where the floor had been cleared and a live band had begun playing. Wedding guests were already lined up around the floor in anticipation of watching the couple's first dance.

"I suppose everyone is waiting on us," Maddox said.

"Tradition is that we dance before we cut the cake," Adeline told him. "Have you had too many cocktails for your feet to keep time with the music?"

He chuckled as he glanced at the giant, four-tiered cake elaborately decorated with flowers and love-birds. "No. I'm thinking I'd like to wash a piece of cake down with some champagne and take the two of us out of here. Far away from this crowd. But you say it's tradition, and we don't want to disappoint our family and friends."

Taking her by the hand, he led her onto the dance floor, and the band immediately started playing a song Adeline had picked out especially for them to dance to. It was a slow, romantic tune, and he took advantage of it by holding his new wife close to him and resting his cheek against her hair.

"This has been an incredible day," he said. "I think getting married has done something to me."

"You don't look sick. So whatever it's done to you, it can't be all bad."

He nuzzled his nose in her soft hair and remembered how he had felt when he'd lifted the veil from her beautiful face and kissed her lips. In that moment, he'd felt transported, and he wasn't at all sure his senses had yet made it back to earth. All he could think about was whisking her away to some secluded place where he could make slow, passionate love to her.

"Nothing bad," he said. "Just different."

Her fingers tightened on his. "You were right, Maddox, when you promised me you'd give me a dream wedding. This has been everything I ever wished for and more. It's a day I'll remember for the rest of my life."

And what about her second marriage, he wondered. The one she would eventually have with a man she really loved. Would it be a dreamy, romantic event?

No. Now wasn't the time to allow his thoughts to go down that path. As long as they remained married, she couldn't have that other man. Maybe that explained why the weight of the gold band on his left hand felt oddly comforting.

Reading. Going for walks. Shopping. Taking long naps. What else was a woman supposed to do on her honeymoon?

Adeline's sigh was heavy as she gazed out the window from their plush hotel suite in downtown Reno, Nevada. For the past few days, she'd spent a ridiculous amount of time staring out at the beautiful view of the Truckee River and the walking path running adjacent to its banks. For the most part, the weather had been mild and sunny, and she'd watched dozens of people enjoying the picturesque walkway. Especially the couples who strolled hand in hand, or with their arms linked, or one arm thrown around their loved one's shoulders or waist. She'd be willing to bet none of those couples had been faking their affection for each other. And in these past days, she'd had to admit to herself that nothing about the deep attraction she felt for her husband was pretense. Being near him only made her want to touch him in all the ways a wife could touch her husband. She wanted them to share hungry kisses. She wanted to feel his hard body beneath her hands and taste his skin. And most of all, she wanted them to be connected in the most basic way two people could love each other.

Turning away from the window, she tried to stem the resentment that had started growing inside her almost as soon as their plane had touched down in the biggest little city in the world.

Of course, she hadn't known what to expect from Maddox on their honeymoon. How could she? Their marriage made unorthodox look normal. And yes, she'd stipulated no sex during their time together as man and wife. But that hardly meant he was supposed to ignore her completely. Or that she couldn't hope their relationship could turn into a real one.

On their wedding day, he'd held her and kissed her as though he'd actually meant it. He'd behaved as if he was thrilled to have her in his arms. Even on the plane here to Reno, he'd been attentive and companionable. But the moment they'd walked into this hotel room, he'd turned into a cool stranger, and his behavior hadn't changed during their entire stay. She'd never felt so ignored and lonely in her life. And she'd reached the end of her rope with his indifference.

She'd thrown a dress and a pair of high heels onto the king-size bed and was about to change out of her jeans when she heard Maddox's access card clicking in the door lock.

Pausing, she watched him enter the room, then remove his cowboy hat and lay it on the cushion of an armchair. She had no idea what he'd been doing for most of the afternoon, but from the pinched look on his cheeks, he'd been out in the cold air.

"Have a nice time?"

Without glancing in her direction, he shrugged out of his coat. "So-so. I visited a well-known ranch with cutting horses for sale. I promised Dad I'd take a look while I was here—if I had the time."

Time? If she wasn't so angry, she would've laughed. The days had crawled by as she hunted for something to do to keep her busy, and she knew for certain he'd been doing the same.

"You know, I might have enjoyed seeing the horses, too. Or didn't that cross your mind?" she asked, unable to keep the sarcasm from her voice.

Frowning, he walked over to the opposite side of the bed from her. Even though they had both slept in the king-sized bed, each had remained on their respective sides of the mattress. The only time he was actually close to her was when they shared a meal at the same table.

"Before I left after lunch, I asked if you wanted to go out, remember? But you were too busy sulking to give me a straight answer. Or maybe you were acting. I'm not sure anymore."

Actually, Adeline had told him to go on without

her, because she'd known he hadn't really wanted her company. He'd merely asked her in order to save himself from looking like a total jerk.

"Acting?" Her laugh was a sound of pure mockery. "Look who's talking. Everything you do and say is as phony as a three-dollar bill!"

He drew in a deep breath and pointed to the dress on the bed. "What are you doing with that?"

"I'm going to wear it—out. Since this is our last night here in Reno, I decided to make the most of it."

"Oh? Where are you going?"

Did he really care? He might as well have asked some stranger on the street, she thought angrily.

"To the Gold Rush casino," she told him. "Since the place is only a short walk from here, I won't have to call a cab."

"The Gold Rush!" His brows shot up, and then his eyes narrowed to speculative slits. "What are you going to do there—find yourself a man?"

One thing was for certain, he knew just the right buttons to push to ignite her temper and feed the flames until they were red-hot.

Faking the coolest voice she could summon, she said, "Why not? I'm on my honeymoon. I should have a man's company, don't you think?"

He stared at her in stunned fascination. "Are you—" Pausing, he shook his head. "What's come over you?"

Furious, she picked up the high heels and threw them to the floor. "That you even have to ask makes me sick," she muttered through clenched teeth. "I'll tell you what's come over me. Now that we're away from our family and friends, I can see the real you, and it's far different than the show you gave them. But that's only a part of what's become clear to me. That this—this sham marriage of ours is a huge mistake!"

His face turned white, and then just as swiftly, it was flooded with a rush of scarlet heat. "A mistake! I'll tell you what's a mistake! Not doing this from the very start!"

Adeline expected him to stalk off to the closet and start packing his bags to leave. Instead, he skirted around the bed and tugged her straight into his arms.

Stunned, her head flopped back at the same time her palms landed against the middle of his chest.

"Maddox, what is…" Her words trailed away as she watched his mouth descend toward hers.

"Tell me if this is a sham, Adeline."

The moment his lips settled over hers, she was completely lost. For days, even weeks, the hunger to be in his arms and kiss him without an audience, without a thought of pretense, had been clawing at her. She was long past trying to hide her desire. And she was so very tired of keeping up the subterfuge.

Her arms went up and around his neck while her mouth opened wider to better receive the search of his tongue.

Her reaction caused him to groan deep in his throat, and then his arms were crossing against her back, drawing her so tightly against him that her breaths had been reduced to tiny sips.

The kiss went on and on until her knees turned to mush and her ears began to roar with the warning that she was running out of oxygen. But before that happened, Maddox eased his mouth from hers and she managed to open her eyes and meet his smoldering gaze.

"Oh, Maddox, please don't act with me now," she whispered. "I couldn't bear it."

"I have no intentions of acting, sweetheart."

"I thought you didn't want me. I thought you—"

"You need to quit thinking and start feeling," he murmured.

He settled his lips back over hers, and that was all it took to wipe the how or why from her mind. The past few days didn't matter, she realized. Neither did the reason for their marriage. All that really mattered was that he was kissing her hotly and passionately and with no intentions of stopping.

Eventually, his hands reached for the buttons on her satin blouse, and by the time he pushed the garment off her shoulders, she was aching to feel his fingers upon her flesh, to have his palms cup the weight of her breasts.

"I am feeling, Maddox. This. You. It's what I want," she whispered.

Her words seemed to ignite a fire in him, and he removed the rest of her clothing with lightning speed.

Once she was totally nude, he took a moment

to kiss each rosy-brown nipple, but the pleasure that shot through her was short-lived as he quickly straightened away from her and began to shed his own clothing.

Once he'd stripped down to a pair of black boxers, Adeline picked up the dress she'd planned to wear to the casino and tossed it onto a nearby chair.

"I don't need that now," she said.

Growling with pleasure, he snaked an arm around her waist and tugged her down with him onto the wide expanse of mattress. "No, babe. All you need is you and me—together."

Lying face-to-face, he gathered her into the circle of his arms, and Adeline sighed with pleasure as his mouth returned to hers and the heat of his hard body warmed the chill she'd felt before he'd walked into the room.

As the kiss grew deeper, his hands seemed to be everywhere. Meshed in her hair, then down to her back, around to her breasts, then down lower to the V between her thighs.

When he touched her there, a wave of desire washed through her, and instinctively she arched her hips toward the magic his fingers were creating against the intimate flesh.

"Oh, Adeline. I can't forget that I'm your husband." The words were whispered between tiny kisses he was planting down the side of her neck. "I can't quit wanting you to be my wife."

Her head lolled to one side as his lips continued on

their downward path to her breast. "All these days, Maddox, I've been wanting you," she said hoarsely. "But you stayed away."

He lifted his head and met her gaze with his. "Because I've been wanting you. And I was afraid this would happen."

"Afraid? Why?"

A pained expression crossed his face. "Our pact, Adeline. We've broken it."

Her head gently turned back and forth against the mattress. "We're not going to think about our pact tonight. We're not going to worry about what we've broken. We're here together. And for me that's all that matters."

He groaned and then, lowering his head, whispered against her lips, "Yes. Nothing but you and me together."

Sighing softly, Adeline closed the last tiny space between their lips and gave herself up to his hungry kiss.

In a matter of moments, she was lost to his mouth, his hands, the feel of his rock-hard body against hers and the heat of his skin scorching her from head to toe.

Time became nonexistent. For all she knew, it could have been hours or only a few short minutes before he finally removed his boxers and parted her legs. When he entered her with one smooth thrust, the sensation of suddenly having him inside her was so great she wondered if they were levitating above the bed. But then he began to push deeper, driving her hips into the soft mattress with a hunger that stole her breath, and she knew they weren't floating. Oh no. They were bound together, melding into one.

His head dipped downward and his lips connected with her before he finally began to move in the timeless rhythm of love. Fiery need rushed to every cell in her body, and she urgently locked her legs around his hips to match his eager thrusts.

If he made love to her for hours and hours, even days on end, it wouldn't be enough, she realized. And with each passing moment, she strained to give him more of herself, to show him how much she wanted and needed him. More than just this night. She needed him forever.

But as the urgency to quench their desire grew more frenzied, the more she felt herself slipping closer and closer to the edge of no return. His roaming hands finally slipped beneath her buttocks and lifted her so that he was diving as deeply as her body would allow.

She was gripping his sweaty biceps and trying to keep pace with him when all of a sudden she felt something inside her burst, and then she was instantly transformed into a radiant star burning across the night sky.

As the velvety abyss closed around her, she cried out his name, then repeated it over and over like a mantra she couldn't stop.

She was still flying on a euphoric cloud when she

heard him make a guttural sound, and then he was clasping her upper body to his and burying his face in the curve of her neck.

As his body shuddered with relief, she could only think how her life had suddenly and drastically changed.

With Adeline snug against his chest and her face turned away from his, Maddox stared at the back of her head and wondered if she'd fallen asleep. For the past few minutes, since he'd rolled away from her and gathered her close, she hadn't moved or spoken. Nor had he.

He'd decided the connection they'd just shared had been too special to ruin with a trite comment. And the words he'd been thinking and feeling were far too fresh and frightening to say out loud to her, or even to himself.

Oh hell, what was this going to do to him and her and their marriage?

Marriage. The word caused something deep in his chest to twist into an anguished knot. Was he still trying to kid himself into thinking his marriage was genuine?

When he'd been making love to Adeline, it had felt very real and right. But he couldn't begin to guess how she truly felt. Yes, the acting he'd asked her to do was now coming back to haunt him. Because now, when she touched him and spoke the words of longing he wanted to hear, he wasn't sure if it was all still an act, if she was merely keeping up her end of the bargain.

Don't be stupid, Maddox. She hadn't bargained to have sex with you. But she is expecting money to be paid to her as soon as the inheritance is signed over to you. She's merely biding her time, enjoying the ride until everything reaches an end.

Fighting to push the hurtful voice from his head, he picked up a strand of her long hair and lifted it to his nose. She always smelled like flowers and sunshine, and he knew that no matter what happened in their future, he would always remember her scent. Her lovemaking.

Moving closer, he nuzzled his cheek against the crown of her hair and slid a hand down her bare arm.

She stirred and turned toward him, and he was relieved to see a dreamy smile tilting the corners of her lips.

"I thought you'd fallen asleep," he said softly.

"With you lying next to me? Not a chance."

He swiped strands of tangled hair from her face, then pressed his lips to her forehead. "I hope you meant that as a compliment."

"Absolutely."

Her eyes were liquid pools flickering with emotions, but the only one he could clearly decipher was desire. The brown depths were smoldering like coals from a fire that had been burning for days.

"This is our last night in Reno," he told her. "We can still go out if you'd like."

She scooted the lower half of her body close enough to wrap her leg over his. "I can think of plenty of things we can do—right here," she said in a husky voice. "And we won't even have to get dressed to do them."

"Mmm. I like the sound of that."

Sliding an arm around her waist, he rolled onto his back and pulled her along until she was lying atop him. From her lofty position, she gave him a wicked smile and then lowered her head until her dark hair was brushing his cheeks and her lips were nibbling his.

Incredibly, he felt desire begin to flare in his loins all over again, and as he allowed the feelings to sweep him away, he blocked all thoughts of tomorrow from his mind.

Later, when they were back home on the Double J, he'd try to figure out what to do about his temporary marriage.

After their night of lovemaking, Adeline had believed their relationship had taken on a new meaning. She'd hoped it was the start of building something real and lasting between them. But in the past ten days, since they'd settled in the family ranch house, Maddox had been attentive and polite whenever they were around his parents and siblings. But once they were alone, he'd reverted to keeping his distance, and it had become achingly apparent that he had no desire to make love to her again.

The only thing that had held Adeline together these past days was the warm treatment Maddox's family had shown to her. They'd accepted her as a true relative and included her in everything that went on with the ranch and their daily lives. But even that would come to an end, she thought sadly, if they discovered the truth about her and Maddox.

"Adeline, I'm really beginning to worry about you and the baby," Trudy said as she eyed her friend's untouched salad. "The food here in Bronco Java and Juice is always delicious, and you're letting your lunch go to waste. Furthermore, you look like you've lost ten pounds. Pounds you couldn't afford to lose."

Adeline bit back a sigh as she glanced around at the noonday crowd. The popular juice bar in Bronco was always crammed at this time of the day, but somehow Trudy had managed to snag a table for them before Adeline had arrived.

"I haven't lost ten pounds." She stabbed a fork into a tiny tomato, and just for an instant Adeline considered telling Trudy how her marriage and pregnancy were both fake. But it was all too humiliating. And like a fool, she continued to hold to the memories of their last night together in Reno. Nothing about those passionate hours in his arms had felt phony. So why was Maddox avoiding her now? Hadn't that night meant anything to him—or was his behavior indicative of the years he'd spent as a freewheeling bachelor?

"I'm a nurse. I know what I see. So eat. We've already been sitting here for twenty minutes," Trudy pointed out. "And I have to be back at the hospital in half an hour."

Adeline began forcing the pieces of crisp vegetables into her mouth. "Okay, nurse. I'll eat."

"So how are you liking living on the Double J?" Trudy asked. "Frankly, I was a bit surprised you two moved in with Maddox's family."

"Actually, I love living with the Johns. And for the time being, it's the best situation for us. The only two houses on the ranch are the main house and Jameson's house, so there's no place for us—until Maddox can build his own house. And that won't be happening for a while yet."

Not when their marriage was slated to end in a year or so, she thought glumly.

"I guess you two living in town would have Maddox too far away from his job on the ranch," Trudy replied.

Adeline nodded. "The commute would be bad. Especially when Maddox and his brothers start work very early in the mornings," she said, then purposely changed the subject. "Tell me about you and Vincent? How's that going?"

A dreamy look appeared in her blue eyes. "He keeps asking me out, so I'm beginning to think he likes my company."

"Yes. But do you like him as much as you first thought you would?"

Trudy released a soft, bubbly laugh. "No. I like

him much, much more. I can't tell you how it feels to have a man at my side who cares about my wants and wishes," she said, then shook her head. "What am I saying? You have Maddox. You know how it feels to be loved and wanted."

Loved. Wanted. Regret sliced through her chest, and then all of a sudden her stomach began to roil.

Flashing Trudy a helpless look, she hurriedly pushed back her chair. "I— Something's wrong. I have to go to the restroom."

She managed to hurry through the crowded tables without colliding with any of the diners, but she barely made it inside the ladies' facilities in time to hang her head over a commode before she lost every bite of food she'd eaten.

The nausea came in waves. But thankfully, as soon as her stomach emptied itself, the sick feeling abated. A few minutes later, after she cleaned up her face and collected herself, she went back to the table to find Trudy in a worried state.

"Adeline, what happened? You look so pale, I'm surprised you haven't fainted."

Adeline took a careful sip of the lemonade she'd ordered to go with her lunch. "I upchucked everything I ate. I don't know what's happening with me. I'm afraid to put anything in my stomach."

Trudy frowned with concern. "If your morning sickness is making it difficult for you to eat or drink, then you should see your doctor. You could become dehydrated."

Morning sickness? Could it be? The suggestion was so stunning she could only stare at Trudy in wonder.

"Adeline? Are you going to be sick again?"

Shaking her head, she gripped the glass of lemonade as her mind continued to whirl with the possibility of her actually carrying Maddox's child. Of course, it was possible, she told herself. She and Maddox had had sex without using any type of birth control. While the two of them had been locked in the throes of passion, Adeline hadn't thought of the risk. Apparently the idea had also slipped Maddox's mind, because he hadn't brought up the subject. And, too, he could've assumed she was either on the Pill or fitted with some sort of birth control device. Which she wasn't. Besides, their honeymoon had supposed to be a sham like their marriage. There wasn't any reason for either of them to pack birth control for the trip.

"No. I'll be fine. Don't worry," she told Trudy. "If this doesn't let up, I'll see my doctor. I promise."

The two women finished what was left of their lunch. However, as soon as Adeline parted from her friend, she drove straight to a drugstore where no one would likely recognize her and purchased a home pregnancy test.

There was no mistaking the plus sign. It was as clear as the morning sky. The confirmation that she truly was pregnant left her so weak-kneed she had to grab hold of the vanity in her and Maddox's private bathroom.

Oh Lord, how was she going to tell him? How was he going to take the news that he, a man who'd never really wanted to marry in the first place, was going to be a father? And with a woman he didn't even love!

Tears rushed to her eyes, but she blinked them back as she carefully concealed the telltale test wand in tissue paper and placed it in the bottom of the trash basket.

No matter how Maddox reacted over the news, she was thrilled to the core to learn she was going to be a mother. Having a child had always been one of her most earnest wishes, and now her wish was coming true. Somehow, in spite of her marriage being untraditional, she was determined to enjoy her pregnancy. Still, she needed time to collect her bearings and her emotions before she shared the information with Maddox.

"Adeline?" Maddox called through the locked bathroom door. "Are you okay in there?"

She dabbed a tissue to her eyes and jabbed it into the pocket of her robe before she opened the door.

"Yes, I'm okay," she told him, her gaze purposely avoiding his. "Why are you still here? I thought you'd be gone by now."

"Wishful thinking?"

The faint sarcasm in his voice made her want to

grind her heel on the toe of his boot. "No. It's just that you've usually gone to the barn before I ever make it to the breakfast table."

He looked away from her and drew in a deep breath. "Sorry, Adeline. I didn't mean to sound short. We—uh—have a lot of work going on here at the ranch right now. And bad weather is predicted in the next few days."

Was that why he'd turned into a cool stranger again? No. With each passing day, she was beginning to get a view of the whole picture. Maddox had needed her as a means to earn the inheritance from his father. Now that the wedding was over and they were back to real life, she was little more than an afterthought to him. She was living on the Double J and sleeping in Maddox's bedroom just to keep up the impression that their marriage was real.

As for the sex they'd indulged in down in Reno, well, that had been nothing but momentary lust for him. And for her? It had only been the beginning of her life.

"I see," she said, then moved past him and into the bedroom, where the covers on their king-size bed were only slightly rumpled from where Adeline had slept hugging one edge of the mattress, while Maddox had remained stuck to the opposite edge. "So did you come to check on me for some reason?"

He walked over to where she stood in front of the dresser mirror. "Yes. Mom sent me after you. She's cooking pancakes for breakfast, and she doesn't want yours to be cold." His expression turned sly as he watched her reach for a hairbrush. "She wants to make sure her grandchild is well nourished—even before it gets here."

Now was the perfect time to give him the news, she thought. She couldn't have a better lead-in to tell him that his baby really was growing in her womb. But she couldn't begin to form the words. In fact, she was having to fight hard just to keep her tears at bay.

"Okay. I—I'll get dressed as quickly as I can. Tell her I'm sorry about being late. I've—uh, been a bit sluggish here lately."

His eyes narrowed. "Are you sick?"

She was sick, all right, Adeline thought, but not the sort of illness he was thinking.

"No. Just tired. These past few weeks have been a whirlwind, and I guess it's all caught up to me."

"Yeah," he said flatly. "It's caught up with me, too."

He walked out of the room, and as he shut the door behind him, Adeline was forced to lean the bulk of her weight against the huge dresser.

Not only was she a fake, she was also a coward, Adeline thought sickly. What else was Maddox going to turn her into before this farce ended?

A mother. That's what he's going to make you, Adeline. So you might as well get ready.

Lifting her head, she studied her image in the mirror and let her memories drift back to when she was getting ready for her wedding and she'd looked in a mirror similar to this once and hoped her marriage would turn out to be the real deal.

She'd gotten the real part, all right. It was rapidly turning into a real nightmare.

As the week unfolded, Maddox did his best to keep his mind on ranch work, especially making sure the cattle were all moved to pastures where the animals could find plenty of shelter from the wind and snow. But he was finding it more and more impossible to focus on anything other than Adeline. And it was becoming obvious to those around him, especially his brothers, that he was miserable.

One of these days you'll get what it's all about, Maddox.

In the past few days, Wes's sage words had come back to him several times. And though he hadn't understood what his friend had meant at the time he'd said them, Maddox was beginning to comprehend them now.

He'd fallen deeply, irrevocably in love with Adeline, but he didn't know what to do about it. Which, in theory, sounded ridiculous. He was married to the woman, for Pete's sake. But she hadn't said *I do* because she was just as deeply and irrevocably in love with him. She'd married him for money. She'd promised to playact and pretend to love him. Just as he'd been pretending. Until the real thing had hit him. Now he figured, even if he could summon up enough nerve to tell her how he really felt about her, she'd never believe him.

He felt as if he was going around in a vicious circle he couldn't break. And keeping his distance from her was only making the situation more unbearable. He could see she was unhappy with his cool behavior, but what was he supposed to do? Take her into his arms and show her all over again how much he wanted her? What was sex going to get him when it came time for them to divorce?

What did sex ever get you, Maddox? You thought it was all you'd ever need from a woman. Why don't you simply take what Adeline offers and enjoy it for as long as you can?

Because, damn it, sex with his wife wasn't enough. It would never be enough.

"What are you doing out here, Maddox? Counting the number of rolled oats in a sack of horse feed?"

The sound of Jameson's voice brought Maddox's head around just in time to see his older brother step into the long feed room, where sacks of grain were stacked all the way to the ceiling.

Maddox shot him a droll look. "Not counting the rolled oats," he said. "Just the sacks. I think Dad needs to order more before the bad weather. Just in case a semi can't make it out here."

"You might be right. I'll mention it to him." Jameson walked deeper into the room and took a seat on an upturned feed bucket. "When I asked you what you were doing out here, I really meant, why aren't you in the house with Adeline? You two are newlyweds, and from what I can see, you've hardly spent any time with her."

Unable to look his brother in the eye, he said, "Adeline hasn't been feeling well. I'm trying to give her quiet time to rest."

"Oh. Guess being pregnant is getting her down."

Maddox inwardly winced. No, being his wife was the reason she was miserable, he could've told Jameson. "I think so. That and all the hullaballoo of the wedding."

"It was quite a ceremony," Jameson agreed. "Mom and Dad are still talking about the impression it made on everyone. Especially the Abernathys and Taylors. So I guess you were right. You have made our parents happy."

Maddox grunted. "Maybe so."

Jameson looked at him. "Maddox, about the wedding—I think we need to talk. If I was wrong about your feelings for Adeline, then I'm sorry for being a jerk. If you really care—"

Feeling sure his raw nerves were about to snap, Maddox cut in sharply, "Yeah, I do really care. And if you're worried about the inheritance—"

"I'm not worried about the inheritance! And that's another thing we need to talk about. I think—"

"I don't want to talk about it tonight. Just leave me alone, will you?"

Before Jameson could ask him what was wrong, Maddox stalked out of the feed room and didn't stop until he'd reached the house.

Since it was well past ten, his parents had retired to their room for the night, and when he reached his own bedroom, he found Adeline had already slipped into bed and turned off the light.

He quietly undressed in the dark and gently lay down on his side of the bed. Across the wide expanse of mattress, Adeline was lying on her side with her face directed toward the wall.

Since he'd entered the room, she hadn't moved or made a sound, yet he sensed she was still awake.

"Adeline?"

"Yes?"

He swallowed hard as the words he wanted to say stuck in his throat. "Uh—nothing. I just wanted to say that I—I talked to Jameson a few minutes ago."

The glow of a yard lamp slanting through the blinds illuminated the room enough for him to see her face had turned toward his.

"And?" she asked dully. "Did he say your father has changed the deed of the ranch?"

He should have known that would be in her thoughts. "No. But he's beginning to think he was wrong about our marriage."

"I'm beginning to think I was wrong about it, too," she said, then turned back to face the wall.

Her words chilled him, and though he wanted to

reach for her, he didn't. Instead, he stared up at the ceiling and told himself he was getting everything he deserved. Especially the pain in his heart.

Chapter Twelve

The next morning, the icy-cold weather that had been predicted to blow in spread over the Double J, bringing cutting winds and spitting snow.

With Maddox and Dawson planning to ride out to check the cattle in the most remote area of the ranch, Maddox decided he needed an extra layer of clothing and hurried back to the house to collect a heavy wool coat from the closet.

When he entered the bedroom, he stopped in his tracks and stared at Adeline, who was standing at the side of the bed, packing a large suitcase with her clothing.

Forcing his voice to remain calm, he asked, "What are you doing?"

Without looking in his direction, she said, "Can't you tell? I'm packing my things. I'm going back to the Lazy L."

His rapid strides carried him to her side. "What are you talking about? Why?"

She dropped the silky garment in her hand and turned to face him. In that moment, in the stark gray light of the room, he could see dark circles under her eyes and lines of fatigue on her face.

He was making her sick, he thought ruefully. Physically and emotionally sick.

"It's about our fake marriage. I can't do it anymore, Maddox. I thought I could. When you first approached me with the whole idea, I believed it would be easy—for the both of us. But it isn't. I hate everything about it. I don't want the money you promised. Keep it. And forget all about that damned pact we made!"

Fury shot through him, and for a second he thought the top of his head was going blow off. "The pact! That's rich. We already broke it, remember?"

Bending her head, she said, "Yes. It's broken— along with my word."

He shook his head. "After all we've gone through, Adeline, how could you do this? Just throw everything away?"

Her head shot up, and she glared at him. "Everything? No, Maddox. We never had anything to lose. At least, not anything of real value."

He jerked off his hat and viciously raked his fingers through his hair. "Nothing of value? Once you leave here, my parents are going to know our marriage was a sham. I'll lose the inheritance!"

Her brown eyes, which were normally warm and inviting, appeared stone-cold as they raked a path over his face. "Maybe you didn't deserve the inheritance in the first place! Has that thought ever entered your mind?"

His mouth fell open, and just as he was about to point out how wrong she was, his thoughts took a complete turn. He didn't know how or when it had happened, but suddenly he understood that all his outrage had nothing to do with him losing the major share of the Double J. He didn't care a whit about the inheritance anymore. All he cared about was Adeline. He didn't want her to leave. He loved her. But trying to convince her of that now would be futile.

"Yeah. I've thought about it. A lot. And I've thought about you, too. I believed you'd stick by me in this, Adeline. For what it's worth, I don't want you to go."

She said, "No. I don't expect you do. Not with all you have at stake."

Her nostrils flared as she turned her attention back to the open suitcase and as he watched her rearrange pieces of clothing, he noticed she'd packed Festus, the stuffed kitty he'd won for her at the Harvest Festival. Apparently, she wasn't ready to give up the cat. Did that mean there was still hope for him?

Maddox was staring at her, his mind whirling for

a solution to make her change her mind, when his cell phone rang.

Seeing the caller was Dawson, he had little choice but to answer. His younger brother was at the horse barn, waiting with two saddled mounts. The two of them had a long ride ahead of them this morning.

"Yeah. I'll be there shortly," he barked into the phone. "Yeah. I can see the snowfall is getting heavier. I'm looking out the window. Whoever told you ranching is easy, anyway? Just hold tight."

He abruptly ended the call, then looked regretfully at Adeline's stiff posture and stubborn expression. Even if he had hours to spare, he could see it wouldn't be enough time to change her mind.

"I have to go," he said.

With grim resignation, she continued to place pieces of clothing in the suitcase. "So do I."

Three days later, Adeline was sitting in a wooden rocker in front of the fireplace in her parents' den, staring regrettably into the flames, when her father's hands rested upon her shoulders.

"The snow has started again," he said. "Looks like we might be in for an early winter. Are you warm enough?"

When Adeline had moved back home, she'd expected her father to raise hell with her. And rightly so. She'd been so headstrong and righteous about marrying Maddox, only to have to admit that she'd made a huge mistake. But thankfully, Louis hadn't accused her of being immature or foolish. He hadn't admonished her for falling in love with the wrong man. He'd simply hugged her and reminded her that broken hearts happened, but he figured she was strong enough to overcome the disappointment.

Adeline had always wanted to think she was a strong woman. But right now she felt helpless and hopeless.

"It's toasty here by the fire," she told him.

Louis sank into a second rocker situated a few feet from hers. "Your mother tells me you had a doctor's appointment this morning. What did he say about you not being able to eat?"

At least with Adeline truly being pregnant now, she didn't have to pretend anymore. Nor would her parents ever have to know that the original announcement of her pregnancy had been a ruse. As for her and Maddox marrying in order to gain the inheritance, that was a secret she intended to keep to herself. Nothing good would come of them learning their daughter had been equally as devious as Maddox. It was enough for them to think her marriage had turned sour for the usual reason of incompatibility.

"He explained the nausea should let up as the baby grows. In the meantime, he wrote a prescription that should help me get past the worst."

"That's good. We don't want you or the baby to get sick."

She looked over at him with a bit of wonder.

Rather than driving a wedge between her and her father, her marriage and the coming baby had ultimately drawn the two of them closer together. She supposed that was plenty to feel grateful about.

"Dad, I've been so preoccupied since I moved back, I'm not sure about any of the things I've said to you and Mom. But I'm fully aware of what I'm saying now. And I want you to know how sorry I am that I've disappointed you and let you down."

He held his hands toward the warmth of the flames. "No need for you to be thinking about any of that now," he said. "Sometimes the only way a person can learn is from making a mistake. Let's just say we've both learned from this and move on."

Adeline had no idea what Maddox was going to think or want whenever she told him about the pregnancy. But there was one thing she was certain of—she and the baby weren't going to live under the same roof as him.

"Well, just so you'll know, I plan to get a place of my own soon. I realize this is something we've fought long and hard about. And I think I always let you win because—well, deep down I love the Lazy L and living here was the safe path for me to take. Maybe a part of me realized I wasn't quite ready to be out on my own. But I want to believe I've grown up considerably in the past several weeks. Now, I want to stand on my own two feet, Dad, and take care of myself and my baby."

He opened his mouth as though he was about

to utter a loud protest, but he must've had second thoughts. His expression quickly softened, and then he shook his head.

"We'll talk about that later, Adeline. Right now you need to concentrate on feeling better."

How could she begin to feel better when her heart, her very soul was aching for Maddox? Not the Maddox who'd grown distant and cold. She wanted the man she'd first met at DJ's Deluxe, the one who'd laughed and kissed her with abandon, the same man who'd made hot, passionate love to her in Reno. But Adeline had a horrible feeling she'd never see that Maddox again.

Later that night, the kitchen on the Double J was quiet when Maddox came in from the barn and shook the snow from his coat and hat. As he hung the items on a rack next to the door, he glanced over at a row of cabinets where a night-light illuminated the counter. The surface had been wiped clean, and the table where the family ate the majority of their meals was covered with a crocheted runner. An orange cookie jar shaped like a jack-o'-lantern sat in the middle. At this time of the year, his mother usually kept the container filled with gingersnaps.

The only sign that the family had already had dinner was the faint scent of Swiss steak. Since his mother knew that was one of Maddox's favorite dishes, she must've have cooked it to entice him to eat.

She'd probably been disappointed when he hadn't shown up at the dinner table. Which wasn't his intention. The last thing he wanted to do was worry his mother. But facing his family right now was worse than riding ten miles in a blizzard. Since Adeline had packed up and left the ranch, he'd spent the past three evenings rubbing down every saddle on the Double J with neat's-foot oil, even the ones that hadn't needed it.

"Maddox? Is that you, son?"

Turning at the sound of his mother's voice, he watched her enter the kitchen, carrying a coffee cup. Even though the hour wasn't all that late, Mimi had already changed into a long, fuzzy robe and slippers.

"Yeah. It's me, Mom." He gestured to her robe. "Are you and Dad already getting ready for bed?"

"No. I've had a long day. I just wanted to get comfortable and sit by the fire. Why don't you join us?" she asked, then shook her head. "Better yet, let me heat some of the leftovers for you. We had Swiss steak. One of your favorites."

"Thanks, Mom. But I think I'll just drink some milk and call it good."

Frowning with disapproval, she said, "You've been working outdoors in this bad weather for most of the day, and you hardly ate much breakfast. Are you trying to make yourself ill?"

He scowled at her. "No. I just don't feel like putting a bunch of heavy food in my stomach right now."

When she took him by the arm and sat him down at the table, Maddox didn't have the heart to resist.

"Okay. Nothing heavy," she told him. "Only I expect you to eat what I give you. It'll make your mother happy."

She went over to the cabinet, and after rustling around for a minute or two, she returned with a small plate of pumpkin bread and a tall glass of milk.

"Thanks, Mom."

She eased into the chair next to him, and after he ate a few bites of the sweet bread, he looked over at her. For now Randall and Mimi knew nothing about his scheme to win the inheritance. When Adeline had left, she'd simply told them she was feeling over-whelmed and needed time to think. Maddox hadn't had the heart—or the courage—to give his parents the truth of the matter. He figured in a few more days they'd realize their daughter-in-law had no in-tentions of coming home.

Trying to shake away the dismal thought, Mad-dox said, "The house is quiet. Where's Dawson and Charity?"

"Charity left earlier in the day for a date with Nick. And you know Dawson. Snow and sleet aren't going to keep him from going into town. I think he was going to Doug's to play pool and have a beer with some of the guys. I told him to be sure not to sit on the haunted stool—especially in this icy weather."

Maddox grunted. "You don't believe in that su-perstitious stuff, do you?"

"Not really. But you can't walk down any street in Bronco without seeing a flyer about Bobby Stone. Makes you wonder if there might be something to the whole legend."

Maddox was suddenly remembering the night of the Harvest Festival dance. A crowd had gathered around Winona to hear her thoughts on the subject, and Adeline had been a little engrossed with the idea that the old lady could actually receive signals from those who'd passed on.

Marriage is the greatest gift. But it's not to be taken lightly.

When Winona had spoken those words, she'd looked directly at Maddox, and he'd felt them to the core of his being. And yet, here he was, trying to move on with his life as if his marriage wasn't worth the few dollars it had cost to buy the license.

He blew out a heavy breath. "Winona says something is missing about the whole Bobby Stone thing, and she ought to know."

Mimi frowned. "Winona? Have you seen her lately?"

"At the Harvest Festival dance. Adeline and I met her new fiancé, Stanley Sanchez. Nice guy."

He drank some of the milk and forced a few more bites of the bread down his throat. Next to him, he could feel his mother's keen gaze traveling over his face.

"You're a nice guy, too, Maddox," she said gently. "You just don't want to think of yourself in that way."

The odd comment had his gaze swinging over to his mother. "What are you trying to say?"

"Only that I can see you're down on yourself. And you're especially down now that Adeline has gone back to the Lazy L."

A heavy lump suddenly lodged in his throat, and he dropped his gaze back to the small plate in front of him. "I don't want to talk about Adeline."

"No. I don't expect you do."

The censure in his mother's voice struck him hard. "Okay," he said, "I'll just come out and admit it. She went back to her parents' because she doesn't want to live with me."

Mimi hardly looked surprised. "Have you asked yourself why? From what I could see, you didn't give her much reason to want to stay here and live with you."

His mother was hitting him right where it hurt the most. Furthermore, she was doing it on purpose. Maddox should be angry at her for adding to the hurt he'd been carrying around these past few days, but he wasn't. He actually wished things were as they had been when he'd been a little boy and he'd thrown himself into his mother's arms and cried out his misery.

"Oh, Mom, things are so mixed up and messed up. And it's all my fault—all my doing."

"I wouldn't say yours entirely," Mimi said gently. "Have you ever thought about all that Adeline has been through recently? Maybe you should ask yourself how the news of her pregnancy might have affected her."

Maddox couldn't take any more. With a weary groan, he put down his fork and faced his mother head-on.

"Oh, Mom. I might as well come clean with you, because you're eventually going to find out anyway. Adeline isn't pregnant. I made it all up just so we could rush the wedding—so that I could win the inheritance Dad put up for grabs. Now, go ahead and tell me what a heel I am! I know I am. But I love my wife. Truly love her. And now…"

Smiling gently, his mother leaned over and patted his arm. "Maddox, you're not telling me anything I didn't already know."

Maddox's jaw dropped. "You knew we were pretending?"

She let out a short laugh. "Yes. But I could also see something very real building between the two of you. And I'll tell you something else. You need to go to your wife and ask her if she's still pretending to be pregnant."

A loud cough sounded directly behind him and Maddox jerked his head around to see Randall staring at the two of them. And considering the perplexed expression on his face, his father had clearly overheard most of his guilty confession.

Slowly, Maddox stood and faced his father. "Dad—I don't know what to say."

"I think I've already heard most of it," he said. "But go ahead. I'm listening."

Feeling more ashamed than he could ever remember, Maddox swiped a hand over his face and then forced himself to look his father in the eye.

"First of all, please don't feel badly toward Adeline. Faking the marriage and the pregnancy was all my doing. Because I love this ranch—my home—so much that I thought I could do most anything to get the huge share you were offering. But I was wrong. I can't live with the deceit. And I can't live without Adeline. My love for her is real."

Randall studied him for long moments before he shook his head. "We've both been wrong, son. I should've never dangled such a carrot over the heads of my children. I think this has taught us both a lesson."

Maddox was stunned by his father's admission. "Do you really mean that, Dad?"

With a resigned smile, Randall reached over and patted his son's shoulder. "I do mean it. And now I think you'd better do as your mother suggested and ask Adeline about her pregnancy."

Frowning with confusion, he looked at his mother. "What do you mean? Adeline isn't pregnant."

Mimi gave him a pointed smile. "No? Well, she's been fighting nausea for days now. I overheard her in the bathroom being sick. Didn't you notice?"

Pregnant! For real? He vaguely recalled Adeline saying she'd been feeling sluggish. But it had never dawned on him that she might truly be pregnant.

Suddenly he was remembering their night in Reno and the passion they'd shared. He'd been so engulfed with the need to make love to her that birth control had never entered his mind.

The realization that Adeline could be carrying his child and he'd been too blind to notice caused him to groan with regret. "Oh, I've been such a fool. And I don't have any idea how Adeline really feels about me. But I have to go to her."

"Of course you do," Mimi said gently.

"And this time, Maddox, be sure and tell her the truth of your feelings," Randall added.

"I only hope she'll believe the truth." Maddox said, then hurried across the room and grabbed his hat and coat from the rack by the door.

As he levered the hat onto his head, Mimi asked, "Aren't you going to wait until morning?"

He looked back at his parents. "I'm not going to wait another minute," he said, then striding back to them, he kissed his mother's cheek and shook his father's hand. "Thanks, Mom, Dad. And forgive me, will you?"

Shaking his head, Randall nudged his son's shoulder in the direction of the door. "You don't need our forgiveness. You need Adeline's."

Adeline was in her bedroom getting ready for bed when she heard multiple footsteps out in the hallway and then her mother's raised voice.

"If you cared anything about Adeline, you

wouldn't be disturbing her at this time of night! She isn't well, and seeing you will only make her feel worse."

"I'm sorry, Mrs. Longsworth, but it's important that I see my wife and speak with her—now."

The sound of Maddox's voice caused Adeline to freeze with disbelief. What was he doing here?

Snatching up a blue robe from the foot of the bed, she hurriedly slipped it over her silk pajamas. By the time she was wrapping the tie around her waist, her mother was knocking.

"Adeline, there's someone here to see you," Naomi announced.

Drawing in a bracing breath, she lifted her chin and walked over to open the door. Her mother was standing on the threshold, but Adeline's gaze went past her and straight to Maddox. The mere sight of his handsome face swamped her with emotions, and suddenly her hands began to tremble and tears gathered at the back of her eyes.

"Your father and I tried to deter him, but he insists on talking to you tonight," Naomi said to her. "Do you feel up to this?"

Adeline wasn't sure what *this* was, but whatever it was, she had to be up to it. Too much time had already passed. She needed to tell Maddox about the baby.

"It's okay, Mom. I—uh—want to talk with Maddox."

Naomi shot him a disapproving glare before she

said to Adeline, "Your father and I will be downstairs if you need us."

Naomi brushed past Maddox, and Adeline stood waiting by the door for him to enter the room.

"I won't waste time asking why you're here," she said as she closed the door behind him. "I'm sure you're going to tell me."

His presence filled the room as he walked over and placed his hat on an armchair. Adeline tightened the belt on her robe and stood near the foot of the bed.

Moving away from the chair, he closed the short distance between them and looked directly into her eyes. The trembling that had started in her hands was now moving down to her knees.

"I'm here to ask you something," he said flatly. "Are you carrying my child?"

She had no idea how he might have guessed her condition, but it hardly mattered now.

Sighing, she looked away from him. "Yes," she said quietly. "I am pregnant with your baby."

"Then why did you leave?" he demanded. "Why didn't you tell me?"

Her gaze whipped around to meet his. "Because I don't want my child to be raised in a home where the parents are only pretending to love each other! Isn't that enough reason?"

His eyes widened, and then his hands reached out and closed over her shoulders. "Who's doing the pretending? I'm not. I'm in love with you, Adeline. I've spent weeks trying to hide it. But now—you have to believe me."

Staring at him with astonishment, she shook her head. "Why didn't you tell me? All those days you stayed away from me as if I had a contagious disease... My heart was breaking. Couldn't you see how much I cared about you? I—"

Her words broke off as he pulled her into his arms and buried his face in the curve of her neck. "Oh, sweetheart, I'm so sorry. I never knew what being in love with a woman meant. I didn't know what any of it felt like, and then when I began to realize I was falling in love with you, it scared the hell out of me. We'd already made that damned pact to have a marriage of convenience. I was afraid you'd want to stick to the deal."

Tears began to stream from her eyes, but they were tears of pure joy. "Oh, my darling," she said as she clutched him close. "Why do you think I made love to you in Reno?"

Easing his head back, he looked at her with blank confusion. "Because you like sex?"

She laughed outright. "I do like it—with you."

A wondrous glow filled his eyes. "And now you're going to have our child. Who would've ever dreamed all those plans we made would turn into the real thing? It's incredible."

She pressed her cheek to his. "Maddox, I hope you're not disappointed about the baby. That night I didn't think about birth control. I should've told you

I wasn't on the Pill or anything. But the only thing on my mind was making love with you."

"This isn't your fault, Adeline. It takes two, and I'm equally guilty of not thinking about birth control. But you know, I'm glad both of us were a little thoughtless that night." Laughing with joy, he rained kisses over her face. "My sweet Adeline, I am totally over the moon that you're truly pregnant with our child. You do love me, don't you? This isn't pretend anymore?"

Wrapping her arms around his neck, she kissed him deeply for long moments. When she finally lifted her head, she asked, "Does that feel like make-believe?"

"If it's make-believe, then I can't wait to feel a whole bunch more of it," he said with a devilish grin. "Do you feel up to getting dressed and going home tonight? It's snowing, but the roads are clear."

"Home to the Double J," she repeated. "Somehow, I always felt as if I belonged there with you."

The look in his eyes was soft and tender and full of promises. "I think I knew you belonged there from the very start."

She kissed him again, then flashed him a promising smile. "Give me five minutes and I'll be ready."

Much later that night, after making slow, sweet love to his wife, Maddox cradled her in the warmth of his arms and nuzzled his nose in her hair.

"I've never been on this side of the bed before,"

Adeline murmured as she turned her head just enough to plant a kiss on his cheek. "The view is very nice over here."

"Hmm. Let me rest a few minutes and we'll check out the view from your side of the bed."

She laughed softly, and Maddox thought how much the rich sound filled his heart. He'd been truthful when he'd told Adeline he hadn't known what it meant to love a woman. But he'd learned. Now he couldn't imagine his life without her.

"Speaking of the view, we have a pretty spectacular one here in our bedroom," she said, turning her attention to the wide span of windows on the opposite side of the large room. "We can see the snow falling over the barn where we got married and, beyond it, all the way to the mountains."

He smiled at the memory of how she'd looked when she'd walked down the aisle and straight to him. He'd felt like he'd been standing in a dream. Now his dream had come true right here in his arms.

"The barn is back to being just a plain old barn with a bunch of haying equipment parked inside," he said. "But the day of our wedding it was a pretty magical place."

"Now I'm a wife and a mother-to-be," she said. "If I felt any happier, I think I'd burst from it."

He rubbed his cheek against the top of her hair. "Hmm. What about the travel agency you wanted to build?"

"Maybe when I'm much, much older and our children are grown," she replied. "Then I'll think about building a business. In the meantime, you and the big family I hope we'll have will be my main focus."

His fingers absently combed through her hair as he glanced around the spacious bedroom. "I've already been doing some planning in my mind and wondering if we should use part of this room to build a nursery. There's a spare bedroom across the hall, but I don't want our baby that far away. What do you think?"

"I think the area over by the windows will make a nice nursery. There's plenty of space for a crib and chest and maybe a dressing table. I'm sure the baby will enjoy the light coming through the windows and, later, the view."

His excitement at the thought of becoming a father was building with each passing minute. "I like your idea. And he or she needs one of those things that dangles bright toys and objects over the crib. What are those called?"

She laughed. "Those things are called mobiles."

"Well, whatever they are, I want it to have ponies and spurs and little cowboy hats on it. Our kid is going to learn about ranching before he ever leaves the crib."

Laughing again, she hugged him tightly. "Oh, Maddox, we're going to have a wonderful future together."

"Yes. And if you ask me, it's pretty damned wonderful right now," he said. "We have so much to look forward to. The holidays are coming soon, and my parents always make a big to-do here on the ranch for Thanksgiving and Christmas. But before that happens, there's the annual Mistletoe Rodeo in Bronco. It'll be a huge attraction. Especially with the Burrises and the Hawkins sisters headlining the event. If you're feeling up to it, we'll go enjoy the fun."

"I am slightly acquainted with the Hawkins sisters. In fact, Mimi and I ran into them at Ever After when I was shopping for my wedding gown." She gave him a coy smile. "Hmm, the rodeo. I'd love to go. And I think I've just found a good reason to buy another pair of cowboy boots. A girl needs more than one pair, you know."

He chuckled. "And what about all those designer high heels in your closet?"

"Oh, I'll wear them when we go somewhere that requires us to be duded up. Otherwise, I'm going to be a real rancher's wife."

Raising up on his elbow, he smiled down at her. "Adeline, I love you."

"I love you, too."

"Good. Because I have something else to tell you."

Her lashes fluttered as she looked up at him. "Should I be worried?"

He leaned down and pressed a kiss to the tip of her nose. "No. I'm hoping you'll be happy. I had a long talk with Jameson this morning about the inheritance of the Double J. We've both agreed that the fairest and best thing for us to do is to make sure all

four of us siblings have an equal share in the ranch.
And we're going to make sure Dad understands how
we feel."

Her lips formed a perfectly beautiful O. "Maddox, I'm so happy. I couldn't be prouder of you. I
only hope you don't feel like you've lost in the deal."

"Lost?" Growling with pleasure, he picked her up
and scooted the both of them to the opposite side of
the bed. "Are you kidding? I won the jackpot—you
and our baby."

She glanced around her. "What are we doing over
here?"

"Checking out the view. Remember?"

The corners of her lips tilted into a wicked smile.
"Come here, cowboy."

Closing his eyes, he lowered his mouth to hers,
and for the next half hour he showed her a picture
of their future together.

* * * * *